OFF THE EDGE!

"Hey!" Frank called up as loudly as he could to the top of the canyon.

Joe and the two men looked down at Frank.

"Let him go!" Frank called, his voice echoing against the vast canyon wall. "We know exactly who you are! If anything happens to him, I guarantee you guys will sleep in prison tonight!"

A moment passed. Frank saw sunlight glint off the glasses both men were wearing.

"Let sleeping scientists lie!" the man in gray shouted down, his voice also echoing. "Do you understand? In other words, get out of town by nightfall—or else!"

Then the man in blue grabbed Joe and gave him a hard shove—right over the edge of the cliff!

Books in THE HARDY BOYS CASEFILES™ Series

#1	DEAD ON TARGET	#74	ROAD PIRATES
#2	EVIL, INC.	#75	NO WAY OUT
#3	CULT OF CRIME	#76	TAGGED FOR TERROR
#4	THE LAZARUS PLOT	#77	SURVIVAL RUN
#5	EDGE OF DESTRUCTION	#78	THE PACIFIC
#6	THE CROWNING		CONSPIRACY
	TERROR	#79	DANGER UNLIMITED
#7	DEATHGAME	#80	DEAD OF NIGHT
#8	SEE NO EVIL	#81	SHEER TERROR
#9	THE GENIUS THIEVES	#82	POISONED PARADISE
#12	PERFECT GETAWAY	#83	TOXIC REVENGE
#13	THE BORGIA DAGGER	#84	FALSE ALARM
#14	TOO MANY TRAITORS	#85	WINNER TAKE ALL
#29	THICK AS THIEVES	#86	VIRTUAL VILLAINY
#30	THE DEADLIEST DARE	#87	DEAD MAN IN DEADWOOD
#32	BLOOD MONEY	#88	INFERNO OF FEAR
#33	COLLISION COURSE	#89	DARKNESS FALLS
#35	THE DEAD SEASON	#90	DEADLY ENGAGEMENT
#37	DANGER ZONE	#91	HOT WHEELS
#41	HIGHWAY ROBBERY	#92	SABOTAGE AT SEA
#42	THE LAST LAUGH	#93	MISSION: MAYHEM
#44	CASTLE FEAR	#94	A TASTE FOR TERROR
#45	IN SELF-DEFENSE	#95	ILLEGAL PROCEDURE
#46	FOUL PLAY	#96	AGAINST ALL ODDS
#47	FLIGHT INTO DANGER	#97	PURE EVIL
#48	ROCK 'N' REVENGE	#98	MURDER BY MAGIC
#49	DIRTY DEEDS	#99	FRAME-UP
#50	POWER PLAY	#100	TRUE THRILLER
#52	UNCIVIL WAR	#101	PEAK OF DANGER
#53	WEB OF HORROR	#102	WRONG SIDE OF THE
#54	DEEP TROUBLE		LAW
#55	BEYOND THE LAW	#103	CAMPAIGN OF CRIME
#56	HEIGHT OF DANGER	#104	WILD WHEELS
#57	TERROR ON TRACK	#105	LAW OF THE JUNGLE
#60	DEADFALL	#106	SHOCK JOCK
#61	GRAVE DANGER	#107	FAST BREAK
#62	FINAL GAMBIT	#108	BLOWN AWAY
#63	COLD SWEAT	#109	MOMENT OF TRUTH
#64	ENDANGERED SPECIES	#115	CAVE TRAP
#65	NO MERCY	#116	ACTING UP
#66	THE PHOENIX	#117	BLOOD SPORT
	EQUATION	#118	THE LAST LEAP
#69	MAYHEM IN MOTION	#119	THE EMPEROR'S SHIELD
#71	REAL HORROR	#120	SURVIVAL OF THE FITTEST
#73	BAD RAP	#121	ABSOLUTE ZERO

THE HARDY BOYS

CASEFILES™

NO. 121

ABSOLUTE ZERO

FRANKLIN W. DIXON

AN ARCHWAY PAPERBACK
Published by POCKET BOOKS
New York London Toronto Sydney Tokyo Singapore

AN ARCHWAY PAPERBACK *Original*

An Archway Paperback published by
POCKET BOOKS, a division of Simon & Schuster Inc.
1230 Avenue of the Americas, New York, NY 10020

Copyright © 1997 by Simon & Schuster Inc.
Produced by Mega-Books, Inc.

ISBN: 0-671-56121-9

First Archway Paperback printing March 1997

10 9 8 7 6 5 4 3 2 1

THE HARDY BOYS, AN ARCHWAY PAPERBACK and colophon are registered trademarks of Simon & Schuster Inc.

THE HARDY BOYS CASEFILES is a trademark of Simon & Schuster Inc.

Cover photograph from "The Hardy Boys" Series © 1995 Nelvana Limited/Marathon Productions S.A. All rights reserved.

Logo design TM & © 1995 by Nelvana Limited. All rights reserved.

Printed in the U.S.A.

IL 6+

ABSOLUTE ZERO

Chapter

1

A BASEBALL HURTLED with intense speed straight for Joe Hardy's head. Suddenly the ball curved down and outward, zooming straight into the strike zone. Joe stepped forward and swung the bat with all his might.

"Strike one!" a voice behind him boomed.

Joe stepped back from home plate and adjusted his batting helmet. What was I doing? Joe thought to himself. I didn't catch anything that time but a couple of yards of air!

A devious smile formed on the pitcher's lips, which irked Joe all the more because the pitcher just happened to be his brother, Frank. The Hardy brothers were both on the Bayport High School team, but occasionally, in practice sessions, they found themselves facing off against each other.

Frank nodded in response to a signal from the catcher. With dark brown hair and eyes, Frank was the calmer, more methodical of the two brothers. At eighteen, he was a year older than Joe, as well as an inch taller.

Joe returned to the plate, determined to blow the next good pitch off the map. Blond and blue-eyed, he was slightly more muscular than his brother and a good bit more impulsive.

Frank went into his windup, then let the baseball fly. Immediately recognizing Frank's famous fastball, Joe hunched his shoulders, took a stride forward, then put all his power behind the swing.

"Strike two!" the voice behind Joe boomed.

Again Joe stepped away from the plate, this time kicking up a cloud of dust in frustration. Sure, it was just a practice, Joe thought, but Frank struck me out yesterday and I *cannot* let it happen again today! Besides, the spring baseball season was coming up in a few weeks.

Okay, time for a hit, Joe reminded himself, gripping the bat.

"Don't stride so soon!" a voice called to Joe.

Joe turned to see a single spectator sitting in the bleachers. It was a girl he had seen in the school hallways but never met. Chestnut hair fell to her shoulders, and she wore a pair of horn-rimmed glasses. Might as well take her advice, Joe thought. Nothing else seems to be working for me today.

As Joe returned to the plate, he told himself

to delay his batting stride just a beat. Joe recognized the next pitch as a slider and was ready for it.

KAPOW! Joe felt the ball smack his bat dead-center and, with no small amount of pleasure, watched it sail beautifully over the head of the left fielder.

"Great hit, Joe!" Coach Sanderson called as he trotted onto the diamond. "If we had a fence, that would have been over it for sure. Okay, fellas, that's it for the day. I'll see everybody tomorrow."

Joe tossed his helmet into the equipment box and trotted over to the girl in the bleachers. "Thanks for the advice," he said, brushing sweat off his forehead. "You got me a home run."

"You're welcome," the girl said with a wise smile. "My name is Irene Weinhardt." There was an air of intelligence about the girl, and behind the glasses, Joe noticed a pair of sparkling hazel eyes.

"Hi, Irene," he said. "I'm Joe Hardy. So . . . I guess you're a baseball fan."

"Not really," Irene replied. "I just knew that delaying your step would allow you to gauge the ball better. Then, of course, the delay would increase the tension between your upper and lower body, thereby creating a much more explosive swing. That part is just simple physics."

"I see," Joe said, nodding, although he was not really sure he did see. "But if you're not inter-

3

ested in baseball, why were you watching us practice?"

"Actually I came to see you," Irene answered.

"Oh," Joe said, perching a cleated shoe on the stands as though he was Mickey Mantle in his heyday.

"You see, I've got a problem, and Phil Cohen said I should discuss it with either Frank or Joe Hardy. So I've been here waiting for practice to end."

"Lucky hit, bro," Frank said, trotting over to Joe and Irene.

Joe introduced Frank to Irene and then told him, "She's got a little matter she wants to discuss with us."

"How can we help you?" Frank asked Irene.

"Okay," Irene said as both Frank and Joe took a seat on the bleachers. "I'll cut right to the chase. My father is Kenneth Weinhardt. He is, or was, a pretty famous physicist."

"Is or was?" Joe asked, puzzled.

"A month ago he was killed in a car accident," Irene informed the brothers. "Supposedly his car veered off that big cliff that overhangs the bay."

"That's right," Frank said, nodding. "I read about it in the paper. I'm, uh . . . really sorry."

"Thanks." Irene hesitated, looking out across the field, then said, "The thing is, I'm not so sure it was an accident. I know this is going to sound totally crazy, but I think my father might have been kidnapped or murdered."

"Then I take it your father's body was never found," Frank said after a moment.

"That's right," Irene replied. "His car was pulled out of the bay, but he wasn't in it."

"Of course, the current could have carried him away," Joe pointed out. "Irene, what makes you think there was foul play involved?"

"My dad was pretty scatterbrained about a lot of things," Irene said, "but he was an extremely careful driver. If anything, he drove way too slow. The weather was fine that day, and I just can't imagine him driving his car off a cliff."

"Anything else?" Frank asked.

"We just moved here last summer when my dad took a teaching job at Bayport University," Irene explained. "Before that, my dad worked for six years at Los Alamos National Laboratory in New Mexico."

Frank knew Los Alamos was a government-owned facility where cutting-edge scientific research was conducted, much of it in the field of weaponry. In fact, Los Alamos was where the first atomic bomb was created.

"What was your dad working on out there?" Frank asked.

"Not weapons," Irene said, taking off her glasses. "In fact, weapons were part of the reason my dad left Los Alamos. He was working with superconductivity."

Frank had learned in science class that super-conductors were substances that conducted electricity far more efficiently than the conductors commonly in use. Superconductivity was currently a very hot issue in the physics world.

"Why do you say weapons were part of the reason your father left?" Frank asked.

"My dad practiced physics because he loved it and because he thought he could make some useful discoveries," Irene said. "But the government became interested in using his findings for a 'national security' project—a fancy way of saying weapons technology. My dad didn't want to be involved, so he quit his post at Los Alamos and took a professorship."

"So I take it your father's work was somewhat important to the feds," Joe said.

"I believe it was," Irene responded. "But I don't really know the details. While he was at Los Alamos, the government insisted my father keep his work secret. When he left, the feds couldn't boss him around anymore, but they requested he keep his findings quiet. And he did."

"Did he continue his superconductivity work after he left Los Alamos?" Frank asked.

"Not really," Irene replied. "He said he needed a break from it."

"And you think he was either murdered by someone who wanted to squelch his work," Joe said, "or kidnapped by someone who wanted access to it."

"That's correct," Irene said. "This suspicion has been eating at me ever since my father disappeared, but now I'm going to do something about it. I'm a member of the school Physics Club, and we're going on a week-long field trip to Los Alamos starting tomorrow. I figured I'd use the trip to ask some questions out there. Phil, who's a friend of mine, suggested I talk to you guys before I go. He didn't say why, though."

"It's like this," Frank said. "Joe and I don't like to make a big deal out of it, but we do a little detective work now and then."

"Really?" Irene said. "Are you any good?"

"We've solved a few mysteries," Frank replied. "But the fact is, I'm not sure there's much of a case here. You feel your father was murdered or kidnapped simply because he was a careful driver and he was doing some important physics research for the government. That's really not much to go on."

"I know what you're thinking," Irene said, looking away. "That I'm imagining all of this as a way of hanging on to my dad."

"I didn't say that," Frank said.

Irene let out a frustrated breath. "That's what my mom thinks, too. But I'm not going to rest until I know for sure what happened to my father. Frank, Joe, sorry to have bothered you. I guess I'll see you around." Irene climbed down from the bleachers and started walking away.

"Wait!" Frank called, running after Irene with Joe.

"I have to go," Irene said, turning to Frank.

"I have an appointment at six-thirty with an old friend of my dad."

"Who's that?" Frank asked.

"The dean of science and mathematics at the university," Irene said. "I figured he might have some new information about my dad's work."

"Look," Joe said, "why don't we drive out there with you? It wouldn't hurt us to look into this a little further."

"Would that be okay?" Frank asked Irene.

"Yes, thank you," Irene replied.

"Just give us a chance to change out of our sweats," Joe said with a friendly smile.

Soon Joe was steering the Hardys' black van down the highway that ran along the bay. There was a little time before Irene's appointment, and Frank had wanted to see the site of her father's accident. "It's right up here," Irene said, pointing. Joe eased the van off the highway and onto the shoulder, shut down the engine, and then the three climbed out.

For a length of about forty yards, the highway veered into a sharp curve. A metal railing protected cars from the cliff that dropped steeply down to the waters of the bay. By the fading light of the sun, Joe noticed a section of the gray railing was newer than the rest.

"Right here is where his car went off the road," Irene said, running a hand over the railing. "They say my father was driving west."

"It's a treacherous curve," Frank said, studying

8

the highway. "If someone was going a bit too fast or wasn't looking—"

"I told you," Irene interrupted, "my dad was a very cautious driver!" Clearly irritated by Frank's comment, Irene stalked several yards away and leaned on the railing.

Frank and Joe walked a little ways east, the direction from which Weinhardt had approached the accident site.

"Of course," Joe said, eyeing the highway in both directions, "Professor Weinhardt could have been forced off the road by another driver coming the other way. It's a tough curve for two cars to handle at the same time. Watch, I hear another car coming right now."

Frank heard an engine and a moment later saw a maroon sports car cruising into view from the west. He noticed the car was going too fast.

Suddenly Frank heard a piercing squeal of brakes. He saw the sports car swing straight for Irene, who was still standing by the railing.

Over the screech of the brakes, Frank heard Irene scream as the car loomed closer and closer.

Chapter

2

SCREECHING WILDLY, the car spun in a full circle, then straightened itself out and roared away in the direction from which it had come.

As the car zoomed by, Frank caught a brief glimpse of the driver, a man wearing glasses with thick black frames. Frank strained to catch the license plates as well, but the car had already disappeared around the curve.

Then Frank noticed Irene was nowhere in sight.

Joe was already racing over to the railing.

"Hey, give me a hand!" Irene yelled.

Several yards away, Joe saw Irene hanging from the railing with both hands. He realized she had jumped over it to avoid getting hit by the car. Below Irene's kicking legs, the sheer wall of the cliff dropped about seventy feet toward the rolling waves of the bay.

Joe ran to Irene and clamped both his hands over her arms. "I got you," Joe said as Frank ran up. Then both Hardys pulled Irene over the railing and back onto the shoulder.

"Did you see that?" Irene said after a few deep breaths. "Someone was trying to kill me just now!"

"Or at least scare you," Joe said. "Either way, I'd say that was no accident."

"Maybe not," Frank said, leaning on the railing. "But who could have known Irene was here?"

"Who knows?" Irene exploded with exasperation. "Maybe someone's been following me everywhere I go! Maybe someone's tapped my phone! Maybe that crazy driver knows I'm about to start investigating my father's disappearance and wants to stop me. I thought you were a detective, Frank. Don't you know how these things work?"

"Come on," Joe said, heading for the van. "Let's go pay a visit to the dean."

Fifteen minutes later Irene and the Hardys were sitting in Dean Patterson's oak-paneled office. Irene explained her suspicions to the dean, a refined man with gray hair, also explaining that Frank and Joe were friends trying to help her sort things out. The dean sat listening in a leather swivel chair, a finger to his lips.

11

"Did the professor talk to you much about the work he did at Los Alamos?" Frank asked the dean.

"I know about as much as Irene," the dean said, leaning back in his chair. "He was doing significant work in the field of superconductors, but I don't know the specifics. The government asked that Ken keep it all quiet, and he honored that request. The government also tried all sorts of persuasion to keep him on board."

"I imagine other organizations would be interested in Weinhardt's work," Frank mentioned. "Do either of you know if anyone else tried to hire him?"

"A lot of universities pursued my father," Irene said. "And some private companies, too."

"That's right," Dean Patterson agreed. "There was one company in particular Ken told me about, some international outfit that was extremely keen to lure Ken into their lair. They offered him an outrageous salary and all sorts of fringe benefits."

"Do you know the name of the company?" Frank asked, leaning forward.

"Ken wouldn't tell me," the dean answered. "He said they had requested confidentiality."

"Why didn't he accept their offer?" Joe asked.

"Kenneth Weinhardt was a man of pure science," the dean explained. "He wasn't terribly interested in the power his government position provided nor the money the private sector had to offer him. He simply wanted to stretch the boundaries of what we know."

"Dean Patterson," Irene said. "About my dad's disappearance—do *you* think I'm imagining things?"

The dean swiveled his chair, facing the dusky light filtering through a window. "I never mentioned this to anyone because I didn't think there was much to it," the dean said. "But the day before Ken's . . . accident, he told me he had a vague notion someone was following him. Then we both laughed, realizing that was probably absurd. Well, that was the last time I saw Kenneth Weinhardt."

It was dark by the time Irene and the Hardys returned to the van in the campus parking lot. "Okay," Frank told Irene, "I'm starting to think you may be right. The maniac in the sports car, the fact that your father felt he was being followed—it's too much to ignore. Joe and I will do whatever we can to help you investigate this."

"Hey," Joe said to Irene, "do you think we could sign on for the Physics Club field trip to New Mexico? We might find some answers at the Los Alamos lab. You know Mr. Cribb, Frank. You're in his class."

"It's awfully short notice," Frank said. "After all, the group leaves tomorrow."

"I'll call Mr. Cribb as soon as I get home," Irene said, her face shining with a smile. "He's usually pretty flexible. And listen, just knowing you guys care enough to help makes me feel a hundred times better."

At eleven-fifteen the following morning, a 727 lifted off the runway at the Bayport airport and began its long journey west. Frank and Joe were on board, as were Irene, Mr. Cribb, the physics teacher, and the other nine members of the Bayport High School Physics Club. An unlucky total of thirteen, Joe noticed.

Joe was sandwiched in between Ed Questal, a skinny whiz kid, and Tiny Marvelson, a giant of a boy who seldom spoke. Over the steady hum of the airplane's engines, Joe could hear Frank and Irene chatting in the row directly behind. Joe didn't know any of the Physics Club members very well, but he could already see they were an interesting crew.

Joe spent a moment watching Ed glue a tiny computer chip onto a small piece of green plastic. The guy's probably building the world's first portable nuclear reactor, Joe thought. Then he smiled, thinking of how Irene had told Mr. Cribb that he and Frank had a serious interest in physics and wanted very much to join the club for the expedition to Los Alamos. Mr. Cribb consented and made the arrangements. Joe realized that in order to keep up the ruse, he could use a brush-up lesson in superconductivity.

"Hey, Ed," Joe said to the skinny kid. "Catch

me up on the current state of superconductors. In fact, start at the beginning for me."

"Well," Ed said, laying his project in his lap, "as you know, for electricity to get somewhere, it has to travel *through* something. Usually we use copper wires, but anything that electricity travels through is known as a conductor. Except even the best conductors present a problem. The atoms in the conducting substance cause resistance, which decreases some of the electricity's power."

"But obviously that's not the case with superconductors," Joe prompted.

"That's right," Ed said. "A superconductor is a substance that allows electricity to flow through it with absolutely *no* resistance."

"Meaning the electricity can travel faster and more powerfully," Joe guessed.

"Correct," Ed said. "Numerous compounds have been discovered that operate as superconductors. But so far none are right for practical usage."

"Why not?" Joe wondered.

"Because they only work at extremely cold temperatures," Ed pointed out. "The superconductors we currently know of operate at or not significantly above absolute zero."

"And please forgive my ignorance," Joe said, "but what exactly is absolute zero?"

"Absolute zero," the deep voice of Tiny Marvelson spoke up, "is the coldest possible temperature."

"How cold is it?" Joe asked, turning to Tiny.

"Negative four hundred and fifty-nine point four degrees Fahrenheit," Tiny said.

"Brrr," Joe remarked.

At two-thirty Mountain Standard Time, the 727 touched down on a runway in Albuquerque, New Mexico. At the airport, the Physics Club and its two honorary guests, Frank and Joe, boarded a minivan and began the sixty-mile drive to Santa Fe, where the group would be staying for the week. Santa Fe was only a short distance from the Los Alamos Lab.

Through the window, Frank viewed the sprawling desert landscape. Sand-colored mesas dotted with scraggly shrubs swept by the highway. In the distance a majestic range of mountains drew slowly closer, their peaks still topped with snow. Hovering above it all was a vast canvas of luminous blue sky.

It was late afternoon when the van finally cruised into Santa Fe, and before long Mr. Cribb parked in front of La Porta, a historic hotel with a white adobe facade. Mr. Cribb, a thin man of fifty with wispy hair, allowed everyone some free time until they were scheduled to meet for dinner at six.

Frank immediately headed for a nearby library while Joe and Irene wandered into the Plaza, the large square located right outside the hotel. The Plaza contained trees and wrought-iron benches and was surrounded by low buildings, most of them centuries old and also made from adobe, a type of clay found in the southwest. A sizable number of people were milling through the Plaza, and Joe could see they were a mixture of locals and tourists.

"It's a lot colder than back home," Joe said, noticing a distinct chill in the air.

"That's because of the high altitude," Irene explained. "It stays cool here till summer."

Joe and Irene had come to a commemorative obelisk that stood smack in the center of the Plaza. They stopped to read a plaque beneath it. Suddenly someone bumped roughly into Irene, causing her to stagger a few steps. "Hey, watch it," Irene called out.

Joe turned to see the backs of two men walking swiftly away. They both wore sweatshirts, one blue, the other gray. Thinking nothing of it, Joe and Irene spent the next half hour checking out the various shops, art galleries, and restaurants in the Plaza. Finally they headed back for the hotel.

Outside La Porta, Irene handed Joe a business card and said, "Joe, look at this. I just found it in the pocket of my coat. I'm sure it wasn't there earlier. I think that guy who bumped into me put it there."

Joe examined the card. It was from an art gallery in the Plaza, but on the back a message was scrawled in ink: "Let sleeping scientists lie!"

Instinctively Joe looked up and scanned the surrounding area. It didn't take long to spot what he was looking for. Two men lingered outside a restaurant next door to the hotel. They both wore zippered sweatshirts with hoods, one blue, the other gray, and the man in blue had a shoulder bag. Both men wore glasses with thick black frames, and they were obviously watching Joe and Irene.

"Didn't Frank say the man in the sports car wore black glasses?" Irene said, also seeing the men.

"Yes," Joe said, his eyes never leaving the two men.

Then Joe saw the man in gray unzip his jacket, reach inside, and ease out a pistol.

Chapter

3

"CROUCH AND RUN for that car!" Joe said, pulling Irene by the arm. Squatting to make themselves smaller targets, Joe and Irene hurried for an empty car parked in front of the hotel, then hid behind it.

Joe peered around the side of the car. While the man in blue kept a lookout, the man in gray kept the pistol close to his body in such a way that none of the people passing by could see it. Joe knew professionals when he saw them.

"Who are you?" Joe shouted at the men. The two men with black glasses kept walking and didn't reply.

Joe glanced at the hotel's entrance. It was only about twenty feet away, but he and Irene would be exposed for several seconds if they ran for it.

Joe knew that was enough time for a few rapid shots to take them down. He saw the two men stop just short of the hotel grounds, the man in gray still holding his gun to his body. They were close. In daylight, anybody could kill from that range.

"What do we do?" Irene asked, fighting panic.

Joe decided the best tactic would be to call attention to the gun. "Why don't you put that gun away," he yelled to the men. "You might hurt somebody."

A few people passing by turned to look at the two men, but they didn't seem to notice the pistol. The man in gray smiled. Then, very slowly, no rush at all, he returned the gun to the inside of his sweatshirt. The man in blue placed his palms together and tilted his head onto his hands, miming someone going to sleep.

"Maybe we don't want to let sleeping scientists lie!" Joe called to the men. "Why don't you just talk to us instead of acting like idiots."

But the men were already walking away, and Joe watched them disappear among the many pedestrians in the Plaza.

"They want to kill me, don't they?" Irene said as she and Joe emerged from behind the car.

"At the moment I think they're just trying to scare you," Joe said. "They want to persuade you not to investigate your father's disappearance."

"Those hoods and glasses are a pretty good disguise," Irene said, adjusting her own horn-rimmed glasses. "I couldn't make out their faces at all, but they give me the creeps, anyway."

Joe nodded. "They're playing cat-and-mouse with us. Call it a mind game."

"Well, I've got a pretty good mind," Irene said, her hazel eyes flashing with determination. "And this particular game I plan to win!"

Brightly colored piñatas hung from the ceiling of the restaurant where the Physics Club was dining. Joe sat at a table with Irene, Ed, and Tiny, each of them sampling various dishes of Santa Fe–style Mexican food. Tiny was putting away tortillas like there was no tomorrow, while Ed was spending more time tinkering with his little computerized device than actually consuming food.

"So, Ed," Joe asked after taking a bite of his enchilada with green sauce, "what exactly are you constructing there?"

Ed looked up, his face two inches away from the gadget, and said, "It's a transmitting device to use on my older sister. I plant this in her purse and I can monitor her movements from a distance of a quarter mile."

"She'll just love that." Irene smirked, keeping a watchful eye on the door.

"I can tell when she's sneaking in my room to borrow my stuff," Ed said.

Joe glanced at his watch, noting that Frank had been gone almost two hours. Just as Joe was wondering if he should go search for his brother, Frank entered and pulled up a chair beside him.

"How's it going?" Frank said as he picked up a fork and nabbed a piece of enchilada from Joe's plate.

"We're still alive," Joe said. Then, while Ed and Tiny began arguing loudly about black holes, Joe lowered his voice and told Frank about the men in black glasses. Irene listened and Frank kept stealing bites of the enchilada from Joe's plate.

"Well, I stumbled on something interesting," Frank said when Joe was done. "In a back issue of the Los Alamos newspaper, I found an article on a Native American activist named Tom Condor. He and a few of his fellow tribe members have been protesting in the area, and they've gotten a little press over the years."

"What does this have to do with my dad?" Irene asked after eating a spoonful of her green-chili stew.

"Condor was employed as a janitor at the Los Alamos Lab," Frank explained. "One day he stopped Kenneth Weinhardt in the parking lot there and started yelling at him. He caused a big-enough scene to gather a crowd. Finally some guards hauled Condor away, and the next day he was fired from his job."

"What was Condor so mad about?" Joe asked.

"He claimed," Frank said, cutting off another piece of enchilada, "that a project Weinhardt had started was responsible for defiling sacred Native American land. The paper didn't report the details of the project or the land's location."

"Defiling sacred ground is a serious crime, according to Native Americans," Irene pointed out.

"Any idea where we can find this Condor guy?" Joe asked.

"He lives at San Ildefonso Pueblo," Frank said, finishing off the last of Joe's enchilada. "It's just a few miles from Los Alamos. There was even a picture of him in the paper. Maybe we can check him out at some point *mañana.*"

"I think we should," Joe said, sliding his plate to Frank. "Here, try the rice."

At eight-thirty the following morning, Mr. Cribb drove the van across a bridge that ran over a gorge lined with deep green piñon trees. On the other side of the gorge were numerous buildings of different sizes and shapes, most all of them the same shade of beige. This was Los Alamos National Laboratory.

As soon as Mr. Cribb drove onto the lab grounds, a guard in a U.S. Air Force uniform pointed the van to the Administration Building. Here, everyone deboarded the van and went inside for an orientation session.

After half an hour, the members of the Physics Club emerged from the building, each wearing a security pass, a laminated card with a photo ID on it. They were greeted by Dr. Robbins, a middle-aged physicist with bushy eyebrows who was to be their guide for the week.

"Welcome to Los Alamos National Laboratory," Mr. Robbins announced as the students stood in the crisp morning air. "As you know, this is one of the finest scientific research centers in the world."

Ed Questal raised a hand, and Dr. Robbins nodded at him. "Would you say," Ed inquired, "that the primary focus of Los Alamos is still in the area of weapons research?"

"No, I wouldn't," Dr. Robbins countered. "Of course, Los Alamos is most famous for being the birthplace of the atomic bomb. And, yes, much of the work currently done here is related to national security. But nowadays we place far more emphasis on other endeavors, such as physics, geoscience, chemistry, biology, computers. If it's related to science, you can bet someone at Los Alamos is hard at work taking it to the next step."

"Why exactly was this location chosen?" Mr. Cribb asked as he adjusted his bowtie.

"For its isolation," Mr. Robbins said with a sly smile. "In 1943 this place was pretty much the middle of nowhere, which made it perfect for the Manhattan Project. The government needed absolute secrecy around the building of the first atomic bomb. And once the physicists working on the bomb were here, they weren't allowed to leave. The fact is, a lot of them felt as though they were being held prisoner."

"The fact is," Irene whispered to Frank and Joe, "I don't like this place."

"Why not?" Joe asked.

"It brings back bad memories," Irene revealed. "When my dad was here, he was so absorbed in his work, he barely had time for me and my mom. I understood his research was important, but sometimes I got the feeling it was more important to him than his own family. But things got much better when we moved to Bayport."

Frank noticed a few men in civilian clothes coming and going, but he saw no military guards in the vicinity. "As soon as the group starts walking," Frank whispered, "we can peel off. When Mr. Cribb yells at us later, we'll just say we met up with an old friend of Professor Weinhardt."

Dr. Robbins fielded a few more questions, then announced, "Okay, let's get rolling. First stop, the Dual-Axis Radiographic Hydrodynamic Test Facility."

"Cool," Joe heard Tiny Marvelson murmur.

Irene, Frank, and Joe walked a short distance with the group before they dropped to the back and began heading off in a different direction. "My father worked in Tech Area 48," Irene said. "If I'm not mistaken, it's about a half mile this way."

"And you don't anticipate a security problem?" Joe asked, casually glancing around.

"See that big fence way in the distance?" Irene said, pointing. "Beyond there is where the weapons research is conducted. That area is very high-security and they've got guards with machine guns to prove it. But for most of the buildings, the pass we have will be enough to get us in the door. It's not exactly legal but it should work."

Soon Irene and the Hardys came to a beige building marked simply TA 48. They walked inside, nodded to a guard at a desk, then proceeded down a hallway as if they belonged there. Irene stopped at a room marked 5 and knocked. A moment later, the door was opened by a sour-faced young woman who wore her hair in a tight bun.

"Hi," Irene spoke up. "My name is Irene Weinhardt. I'm Kenneth Weinhardt's daughter."

"Excuse me," the woman said, eyeing Frank and Joe, "but were you two given clearance to come in here?"

"Yes," Frank said, fingering the pass clipped to his shirt. "A Dr. Robbins issued us clearance." The woman gave Frank a dubious look.

"Irene?" a man said, approaching the door. He was a kindly-looking man of about sixty. He had white hair, and his Western shirt was embellished with a string tie. "I'm Ralph Owens. I was a good friend of your father's. Please, come in."

Irene and the Hardys stepped into the room. It resembled an ordinary office, consisting mostly of desks, filing cabinets, and lit-up computers.

"It's good to see you, Dr. Owens," Irene said, offering her hand. "I met you a few years ago."

"I didn't recognize you at first," Owens said, taking Irene's hand fondly. "You've grown into such a beautiful young woman. You know, I'm terribly sorry about your father, terribly sorry. But tell me, what brings you back to Los Alamos?"

"Well," Irene said, choosing her words carefully, "I have a few questions about the work my father was doing here at the lab. There are some things I want to know. You see, I have this . . . suspicion that my father's death may not have been a complete accident. Or that he may not be dead at all."

"I see," Owens said, nervously fingering his string tie. "At least, I think I see."

"Ralph," the sour woman interrupted, "I know this is Weinhardt's daughter, but I really don't think you should say anything without obtaining permission."

"This is my colleague, Dr. Bernstein," Owens said, introducing the woman. "I'm afraid she's right. The work we do here is somewhat classified. But I'd be happy to answer a few, well . . . general questions about your father, if that would be of any help."

Frank saw the direction the conversation was going—nowhere. Maybe if they could get Owens alone, or maybe if Frank had pretended to be a cleared scientist, they might have had a better

27

chance. As Irene and Owens continued conversing, Dr. Bernstein watching like a guard dog, Frank realized no one was paying any attention to him.

Quiet as a cat, Frank opened the door and slipped out of the room. He walked down the hallway, glancing at the identifying plates on the doors, finally stopping at a door marked Research Lab 11.

Frank turned the door handle, cracked open the door—then felt himself being jerked into the room by an incredibly powerful force. It was unlike anything he had ever felt before, and he was powerless to stop it.

Chapter

4

FRANK WAS PULLED CLEAR across the room until his wrist smacked up against a metal object sitting on a counter. He saw the object was a large mirror-shiny cylinder, roughly the size of a garbage pail, that protruded from a framework of black metal.

Frank tried to jerk his wrist free, but the cylinder would not give an inch. He realized he was stuck to some sort of super-magnet that had attracted the iron in his wristwatch. He also noticed two young men in white lab coats watching him, one with short hair, the other with a ponytail.

"May we help you?" the short-haired physicist asked without a hint of humor.

"Uh, yeah," Frank said, feeling very stupid with his arm helplessly attached to the magnet. "I just need to, uh . . ."

The ponytailed physicist flipped a switch, and Frank felt the magnet release his watch.

"Thanks," Frank said, glancing around the room. Perched on wide counters that ran around the lab were various high-tech machines, circuitous glass tubes with colored liquids inside, and other perplexing paraphernalia.

"I suppose you're the geothermal physics intern from Cal Tech," the ponytailed one said. "Sam Barkley, right?"

"Right," Frank said, hoping the two physicists would not read the name on his pass.

"You're an hour late, you know," the short-haired one scolded.

"I know, I know," Frank said. "I got a little lost in the, uh . . . complex. Sorry."

"Okay, Sam," the ponytailed one said, sitting on a stool. "Before we put you through your paces, do you have any questions?"

"As a matter of fact, I do," Frank said, sitting on another stool. "One of my professors at Cal Tech was telling me about Kenneth Weinhardt. Did either of you guys work with him?"

"I worked with Weinhardt for a while," the short-haired one said. "Brilliant man. Totally obsessed with his work. But just when things started getting interesting, Weinhardt and his work were moved into another building, on the other side of the fence."

"Why is that?" Frank wondered.

"Apparently," the short-haired physicist said,

"Weinhardt made a discovery that the government thought had some real weapons potential. The brass got real nervous."

"Would you know what that discovery was?" Frank asked.

"Not exactly," the short-haired physicist said. "But rumor has it that he—"

Suddenly there was a sharp knock at the door.

"Come in," the ponytailed physicist called.

Two Air Force guards entered the room, and Frank noticed their gun holsters were unsnapped. "You—come with us," one of the guards said to Frank.

"May I ask what this is about?" Frank asked.

"No," the guard replied.

As the physicists watched in confusion, the two guards escorted Frank out of the room. Outside, the guards put him in a jeep, then drove to another one of the beige buildings. Frank was left sitting on a folding chair in a cheerless room.

After a long wait, a slender man in his mid-thirties breezed into the room and sat in a chair opposite Frank. He wore a stylish suit and highly polished black shoes. His dark hair was slicked back to perfection, and his intense eyes seemed to burn a hole straight through Frank.

"My name is Special Agent Martinez," the man said, holding a clipboard. "I'm with the Federal Bureau of Investigation."

"Nice to meet you," Frank replied. "I'm—"

"Frank Hardy," Martinez interrupted. "You're

31

visiting Los Alamos with the Bayport High School Physics Club. Except you're not really a member of the club. Furthermore, this morning you and your brother, Joe, and a Miss Irene Weinhardt left the group to trespass onto Tech Area 48—which is in direct violation of federal law. Now, tell me, Frank Hardy of Bayport, what were you doing?"

Frank thought a moment, mentally sorting through his options, and decided he would be better off telling the absolute truth.

"Kenneth Weinhardt was supposedly killed a month ago in a car accident," Frank stated. "However, his daughter believes there was foul play involved, and I'm helping her look into this. I was trying to get some information on what Weinhardt was working on here."

"In other words," Martinez said, flicking lint off his suit, "you were only trying to help a friend."

"Correct," Frank said.

"What color are your mother's eyes?" Martinez suddenly asked.

"Blue," Frank answered.

Martinez checked his clipboard, and Frank realized the FBI had created a detailed computer file on him in a matter of minutes.

For the next hour, Martinez grilled Frank, asking every conceivable question. Frank answered them all honestly, knowing Martinez was trying to determine if he was a professional spy or just an overinquisitive teenager. When the questioning was through, Martinez picked up a telephone. "Bring them all in," Martinez spoke into the receiver.

Several minutes later two different guards escorted Irene, Joe, and a very flustered Mr. Cribb into the room. Frank learned they had all been subjected to similar interrogations.

"All right, folks," Martinez announced to the group. "I'm not going to press charges against any of you, but I am revoking clearance passes from Frank, Joe, and Irene. Until I can investigate this matter more fully, you three will not be allowed on the grounds of the Los Alamos National Laboratory. Sorry, kiddos, but that's the way it is. If you three will hand me your passes, please."

The meeting adjourned, and Mr. Cribb, Irene, and the Hardys were escorted outside by the two guards. The group stood silently in front of the beige building for an awkward moment.

"This is certainly a fine mess," Mr. Cribb said.

"I'm very sorry, sir," Frank apologized.

"Apology accepted," Mr. Cribb said with a curt nod. "Irene explained why you and Joe are really here. Though I certainly am not pleased about this, I do understand. Now the question is, what are you three going to do for the rest of the day?"

"Maybe we could go sightseeing," Frank offered.

"In what?" Mr. Cribb inquired.

"The van?" Joe suggested.

"The van," Mr. Cribb repeated dubiously.

"It's either that," Irene said, "or we sit in the parking lot for the rest of the day. I promise we'll have it back here on time and that we won't get into any more trouble. You know me, Mr. Cribb. I'm trustworthy."

"I'll probably lose my teaching license for this," Mr. Cribb said, handing Irene the keys. "Be at the front gate at five o'clock—sharp!"

"Thank you, sir," Joe said with a small salute.

As Mr. Cribb walked away, Frank noticed Ralph Owens hurrying over. "Irene," Owens said after a nod at the two guards, "I'm sorry about all this trouble, but Dr. Bernstein always goes by the book. I'm afraid she's the one who blew the whistle on you folks. Anyway, I wanted to recommend a wonderful restaurant in Santa Fe. The best chili rellenos in town. Here's the name and address."

Owens handed Irene a sheet of paper, gave a little wave, then left as quickly as he came.

Puzzled, Frank watched Irene open the folded sheet of paper. It read, "Meet me at the San Jose mission at 3:30 P.M." After stealing a look at Frank, Irene quickly refolded the paper and slipped it in the front pocket of her jeans.

Moments later Joe was driving the minivan west toward San Ildefonso Pueblo. The trio hoped to have a few words with Tom Condor, the janitor who had confronted Professor Weinhardt in the Los Alamos parking lot.

Frank was gazing out the window at the vast sky and rocky mesas. He glimpsed a large bird soaring against the clouds that he realized was an eagle.

"Frank, what are you thinking?" Irene asked.

"Irene," Frank said, "back at Los Alamos you said something interesting. You said sometimes you thought your father cared more about his research than his own family. Then in Lab 11, this guy told me the government moved your father into another building to keep his work even more classified."

"What are you driving at?" Joe asked.

"This is way off the wall," Frank said, "but I wonder if there's any chance Professor Weinhardt allowed the government to fake his death so he could carry on his work in complete secrecy."

"My dad would never do that without telling me and my mom," Irene argued. "Especially not for the purpose of developing weapons. Forget it!"

"Well, you know your father better than me," Frank said. "But still . . ."

"What?" Irene said. "Say it."

"Scientists are ambitious people," Frank pointed out. "If you give one a chance to make an earth-shattering discovery, well, that's a hard thing to resist. Somehow I doubt the government would send those men with glasses, but then, well . . ." Frank's eyes returned to the eagle.

Soon Joe parked the van alongside a group of other cars outside San Ildefonso Pueblo. Frank, Joe, and Irene were required to register inside an adobe building that served as a visitors' center. They were also given a pamphlet that explained the pueblo's visiting rules. After briefly looking at some of the glazed black pottery for sale, the trio stepped outside and entered another world.

About fifty brownish adobe structures stood circled around a large central plaza of dirt. Some of the adobe structures stood independently while others were stacked several stories on top of each other in a manner resembling an ancient apartment complex. The various levels were connected by wooden ladders, and the buildings had doors painted a variety of colors.

"The Puebloan people have always lived in close-knit communities," Irene told Joe, "and the word *pueblo* actually translates as 'village.' "

A few tourists and a small number of villagers were moving around the plaza. Frank noticed several village women, wearing vividly colored dresses and plenty of silver jewelry, working at large clay ovens in the ground. Wisps of smoke curled upward from the ovens.

"They're baking bread," Frank said.

"The same way they've done it for centuries," Irene added. "As much as possible, these people try to maintain their traditional lifestyle. Although if you stepped inside one of those adobe homes, you'd find telephones, stereo systems, and television . . . uh-oh."

"What?" Frank asked, noticing Irene was looking nervously around.

"Where's your brother?" Irene asked.

Frank scanned the area, spotting Joe across the plaza. He was standing beside a large hole in the ground with a wooden ladder rising out of it. "There he is," Frank said, pointing.

Then Frank saw that the women baking bread were also pointing at Joe, and they were now chattering angrily in their native language.

"Come on," Irene said, leading Frank toward the hole in the ground. "Joe shouldn't be there."

Suddenly Frank saw a Native American man enter the plaza and head in Joe's direction. He wore jeans, a denim jacket, and a gray cowboy hat, under which his long black hair flapped in the wind. When Frank caught a look at the man's face, it seemed familiar somehow.

A beat later Frank realized he had seen the face yesterday in the newspaper article he'd read. It was Tom Condor!

Chapter

5

As FRANK PICKED UP his pace, he realized that Condor was making directly for Joe. When he reached him, he grabbed Joe by the arm and swiftly spun him around. Joe, caught off guard, lost his footing and hit the dirt. He bounced up and found himself staring into the dark eyes of Tom Condor.

"What's the big idea?" Joe shouted at Condor.

"It was a warning to get away from that hole in the ground," Condor said.

"It's a kiva," Irene said as she and Frank approached. "A holy chamber. A place where they conduct religious ceremonies."

Condor glanced at Irene and Frank before turning back to Joe. "If you had taken the trouble to read the pamphlet you were given," Condor said, "you would have known to stay away from the kiva."

"I'm sorry," Joe said, meaning it. "I should have been more respectful."

Condor nodded, then started to walk away.

"Wait," Frank called. "You're Tom Condor, aren't you?"

"Who wants to know?" Condor asked, turning.

"My name is Frank Hardy. That guy you grabbed is my brother, Joe. And this is Irene Weinhardt."

"Weinhardt?" Condor said, his eyes playing over Irene. "By any chance are you . . ."

"I'm Kenneth Weinhardt's daughter," Irene said. "My father is dead, or at least he might be. He disappeared recently under mysterious circumstances. I'm trying to figure out what happened to him."

"Yeah?" Condor said with a scowl. "So what does this have to do with me?"

"We know you had an argument with Weinhardt one day in the Los Alamos parking lot," Frank said. "It had something to do with land being defiled."

"That's right," Condor replied. "But I didn't kill him, if that's what you're getting at."

"I didn't say you did," Frank said calmly. "Could you tell us a little about the land? Where is it? What happened to it?"

Condor stared at the trio a moment. "Do any of you know Bandelier?" Condor asked finally.

"Sure," Irene said.

"Meet me there in half an hour," Condor instructed. "By Long House. You'll get your explanation there." Tom Condor hurried across the plaza, giving a wave to the women baking bread.

"What's Bandelier?" Joe asked.

"It's a park that contains Native American ruins," Irene explained.

"That must be the land in question," Frank said, watching the oven smoke curl into the sky.

"Or maybe it's just a convenient place for him to trap us," Joe said, seeing Condor disappear inside an adobe house.

Twenty minutes later Joe pulled the van into the visitors' parking lot at Bandelier National Monument. The Hardys and Irene climbed out, paid a small fee at an admission booth, and entered the actual park grounds.

A trail led the trio into the center of a magnificent canyon. One side of the canyon wall and most of the canyon floor were lushly covered with piñon trees, but the other side of the canyon was a steeply rising wall of salmon-colored volcanic rock. As he walked along the trail, Joe saw a few other people checking out the park, but not many. He figured Bandelier got much more crowded in the summer months.

Soon Joe saw the first of the ruins. On the grassy floor of the canyon, the skeleton shapes of ancient homes stood around a circular plaza. Joe also noticed a large round hole in the ground, which he assumed was a kiva.

"Look over there," Irene said, a little way down the trail. Frank saw hundreds of dark holes carved into the rocky side of the cliff. "Those are caves where people used to live."

Still farther down the trail, the trio came to the most impressive sight yet. Hundreds of holes and indentations in the side of the cliff indicated that the site was once a massive complex of homes. Above the ghost village, the sheer canyon wall soared up into the sky.

"Good, you made it," came a voice. Joe turned to see Tom Condor standing beside him.

"About eight hundred years ago this complex was built by my ancestors," Condor said, his eyes watching the ruins as if he still saw people roaming in and out of the rooms. "The people who lived here are known as the Anasazi. It means the 'ancient ones.' They were a peaceful people, farmers mostly."

"What happened to them?" Joe asked.

"They left eventually," Condor explained. "No one really knows why. Maybe drought, disease, war. Then a white man stumbled on the site a hundred years ago, and the U.S. government turned it into a national park."

"What does this have to do with my father?" Irene asked eagerly.

"One day last year," Condor said, moving closer to the ruins, "I came out here and discovered the place had been temporarily closed. No one said why, but I discovered it had something to do with the Los Alamos Lab. I was a janitor there, so I did some snooping. It wasn't too hard. I had keys and I know a little about computers."

"What did you find?" Frank asked.

"Apparently," Condor continued, "some rare mineral or element is contained in these cliffs. I don't know what it was, but they called it by a code name: Flash. It turns out Kenneth Weinhardt was working on a project that required large amounts of Flash."

"And that's why the park was closed?" Joe said.

"Yeah," Condor said, bitterness creeping into his words. "The Los Alamos people brought in their equipment, and for several weeks they went digging all around here, looking for that stuff. I snuck in one day to watch. Those workmen were digging under the ruins, through the caves, inside the kivas, ripping apart the sacred ground of my ancestors."

As he listened, Frank noticed a serpent carved into the stone wall of the cliff.

"I was furious," Condor said, kneeling to touch the stone foundation of one of the rooms. "So I waited for Weinhardt one day in the parking lot. I told him I didn't care how important his little project was; no one has the right to go stomping on the spirits of my people."

"What did he say?" Irene asked, truly curious.

"He was somewhat apologetic," Condor revealed. "But then he looked me square in the eye and said there is no way to stop progress. Man was meant to bend the earth to his will and, well, sometimes things like this happen. Never has anyone made me so angry. I lost it. Yelled my head off. Got fired for it."

"I see," Frank said.

"If you white kids want to think I'm just a vicious Indian scalper," Condor said, "I guess I can't stop you. But I'm telling you, after that day, I never set eyes on Kenneth Weinhardt again." Condor rose to his feet and brushed his palms together. "Well, that's all I have to say about it. Enjoy your stay at Bandelier, folks, courtesy of the United States Government."

Before anyone could respond, Condor was walking toward the trees on the canyon floor.

"What do you think?" Joe asked the others.

"Weinhardt didn't do the actual defiling," Frank said, "but apparently Condor holds him somewhat responsible. Especially after that crack in the parking lot. Maybe Condor felt the laws of his tribe demanded someone die for this crime and he picked Weinhardt."

"You said Condor works with other activists," Irene mentioned. "Maybe some of the others could be the men in glasses. They could have tapped my phone, discovered I was on my father's trail, and come after me."

Joe was listening but also watching something

43

farther along the canyon wall. "Frank," Joe said, "take a real casual look behind you in a sec."

After a moment Frank turned as if admiring the scenery. He noticed a redheaded man in a bomber jacket standing in the gorge, taking photographs of the ruins. "He's been standing there almost the whole time we've been here," Joe explained.

"He's probably just a tourist snapping pictures," Frank said. "But it's pretty empty out here. We should all be extremely careful."

"It's now two-oh-five," Irene said. "We've got some time before we're scheduled to meet Owens. Do you guys want to have a look at the caves?"

"Definitely," Frank said.

Soon Frank, Joe, and Irene were following a trail that angled its way up the side of the rocky cliff. They came to a level stretch of ground where a row of caves were located. Some of the caves had wooden ladders leading to them. Irene and Frank climbed a ladder and disappeared inside a cave. Joe lingered outside to examine the area from a higher vantage point. As he admired the nearby mountains that lay against a gigantic blue sky, Joe took a deep breath of the pine-scented air.

Suddenly Joe felt an object poke into his back. It felt like the barrel of a gun. "Don't make a sound" came a low voice. Using his peripheral vision, Joe noticed there were two men standing behind him, one wearing a blue sweatshirt, the other gray.

"You did not take our advice" came another voice. "That was a big mistake. Start walking."

Frank had to stoop as he moved through the cave's shadowy interior. Enough sunlight streamed into the cave for him to see the ceiling was blackened from smoke. "Why did they have both caves and free-standing homes?" Frank asked.

"We're not sure," Irene answered. "Everything about the Anasazi is a mystery. Why they came here. How they built their dwellings. Why they left. And especially, where they went."

After several minutes of exploring the cave, Frank said, "Let's go find Joe. I think the three of us should stick together out here."

After Frank and Irene climbed out of the cave, they stood in the sunlight, scanning the area for Joe. But he was nowhere in sight. Frank saw a few people moving along the trail far below, but there didn't seem to be anyone else in the vicinity.

"Joe!" Frank called out. "Joe, where are you?" There was no answer but the breeze rustling through the piñon trees across the gorge.

"Let's check the other caves," Irene suggested. There were about a dozen other caves with ladders leading up to them, and Frank and Irene

45

checked every single one, still finding no trace of Joe.

Frank was growing more and more concerned. Perched on a ladder, he scanned up and down the splendid canyon vista. Then he saw three figures angling up the part of the trail that led to the top of the canyon.

Squinting against the bright sun, Frank could see two of the figures wore sweatshirts, one blue, one gray. When he saw the third figure wore a red jacket, he realized it was Joe. Irene saw them, too.

Frank and Irene moved as quickly as they could up the steeply rising trail. Soon their breathing became labored due to the high-altitude thin air. Rocks were sliding away under Frank's feet, telling him he was going too fast, but he had no choice. He found himself growing angry at Joe for being careless, but then he realized that was a waste of energy. Just keep climbing, Frank told himself.

Suddenly Frank heard a thud. He spun around to see Irene sliding down the trail, rocks and dust tumbling with her. Frank ran down the slope to help.

"Sorry," Irene said as Frank pulled her to her feet. "It won't happen again."

When Frank glanced up, he could see Joe and the two men standing at the very top of the cliff. All three were lingering near the cliff's edge for some reason. They were a dizzying distance above the canyon floor, probably six hundred feet, and still a good way above Frank and Irene.

Frank realized Joe might be gone or dead by the time he and Irene made it to the top. He had to do something—fast.

"Hey!" Frank called up as loudly as he could. Joe and the two men looked down at Frank.

"Let him go!" Frank called, his voice echoing against the vast canyon wall. "We know exactly who you are! If anything happens to him, I guarantee you guys will sleep in prison tonight!"

A moment passed. Frank saw sunlight glint off the glasses both men were wearing.

"Let sleeping scientists lie!" the man in gray shouted down, his voice also echoing. "Do you understand? In other words, get out of town by nightfall—or else!"

Then the man in blue grabbed Joe and gave him a hard shove—right over the edge of the cliff!

Chapter

6

IRENE GASPED with horror.

Paralyzed, Frank watched Joe plummet straight down the sheer face of the cliff, his arms flailing wildly above his head. Suddenly Joe jerked to a stop a third of the way down the cliff. Then his body bounced up and down several times, the fall halted by some unseen force.

"What happened?" Irene said, barely able to speak.

"It looks like they tethered Joe to a bungee cord," Frank said, watching Joe dangle in midair. The edge Joe had been thrown from jutted out enough so that he had not collided against the cliff's wall. Looking up, Frank noticed the two men with glasses were gone, or at least out of view.

Frank and Irene scrambled up the trail as fast as they could, soon coming to a ledge not far from the dangling Joe. With Irene holding on to him, Frank reached for Joe while Joe swung his body toward him. After a few misses, Frank managed to grab his brother and pull him onto the ledge.

"They nabbed me right outside the cave," Joe explained as he untied the cord wrapped around his middle. "I thought I was dead at first, but I guess this was just another attempt to frighten us. The guy in blue had a bungee cord in his shoulder bag. He tied one end around my waist and the other around a boulder. That fall was plenty scary for me, but I'm sure it was even scarier for you guys."

"Scared? Us?" Irene said. She gave Joe a quick hug.

"Folks like us don't get scared," Frank said as he slapped Joe on the back.

"Sometimes I wonder why we do this," Joe said, stealing a look down the sheer wall of the canyon.

After returning to the van, Frank, Joe, and Irene drove a short distance to another national park, Jemez State Monument. They moved through the grassy grounds, which were surrounded by low green hills, and came finally to the remains of the San Jose mission, the spot designated for the rendezvous with Ralph Owens.

The stone structure was partially crumbling in places but retained its original shape from the seventeenth century. There was nothing around except several piñon trees, the late afternoon sun forming long shadows from their trunks.

After a few minutes of waiting, Joe saw Ralph Owens walking toward the mission at a quick pace. "Hi," Owens said as he reached the group. "To be honest, I'm not real comfortable being here, so we should make this as brief as possible. Tell me, Irene, how can I help you?"

"Dr. Owens," Irene said, "I know something awful has happened to my father, and I'm trying to figure out what that might be. To do this, I need to learn whatever I can about my dad's work at Los Alamos."

"I understand," Owens said with a frown.

"Why don't we step into my office?" Joe said, indicating the mission. "It'll be more private."

Joe led the group through a space where a door used to be and they were inside the shell of the mission. There was only empty space where an altar and pews had once been.

"As you folks know," Owens began, "so far we only have superconductors that work at very cold temperatures. Like countless other physicists, Kenneth Weinhardt was searching for something that would superconduct at a far higher temperature. In short, after years of experimentation, he developed a new compound composed mostly of a rare element known as lexanium."

"Flash," Joe said.

"Well, yes," Owens said, surprised Joe knew the code name. "Anyway, the compound Ken developed was able to superconduct at temperatures higher than any previously formed substance. The temperatures were still very cold, but Ken felt he might soon be able to perfect this compound into something that would superconduct at very close to room temperature."

"And then electricity would become both cheaper and more powerful," Frank observed.

"Oh, the benefits of this breakthrough would be overwhelming," Owens pointed out. "It would change the face of computers, communications, travel, space exploration. And, of course, there could be military advantages—especially if the government was able to keep this secret compound to themselves."

"Of course," Irene scoffed.

"As soon as Ken formed this compound," Owens revealed, "his research was bumped up to the highest level of secrecy. That's because the government thought Ken's work could lead to a new generation of weaponry. But this bothered Ken and he soon left Los Alamos because of it. He told me he didn't want to be the creator of the next atomic bomb."

"I can see why the government was so reluctant to let him go," Joe commented.

"Aside from military applications," Frank said, "this breakthrough could also be worth a fortune in the commercial marketplace."

"Dean Patterson at Bayport University said some international company was really after my father," Irene told Owens. "Do you know anything about this?"

"I do," Owens said, nervously touching his string tie. "The company you speak of started pursuing Ken shortly after he made the lexanium discovery. Both Ken and I suspected they found out about it somehow—probably through espionage."

"By any chance," Frank said, "did Weinhardt tell you the company's name?"

Owens cleared his throat. "Yes," he said. "This company requested Ken keep their name and the nature of their offers confidential, but Ken told me all about it. I'm probably the only one who knows. It's an outfit called International Development Engineering Associates. They're also known by the acronym IDEA. They specialize in researching and developing products based on new technology."

"Dr. Owens—" Joe began.

"I'm sorry," Owens interrupted, "but I need to be going now. I guarantee I've told you everything I know about this. I can't say if anything sinister happened to Kenneth Weinhardt or not. But I can say this: His work might have changed the world we live in, and when the stakes are that high, anything is possible."

"Dr. Owens," Irene said, taking the man's hand, "this was a big risk for you and I'm very grateful."

"I wish you the best of luck, Irene," Owens said, giving Irene's hand a squeeze. "I sincerely hope you find the truth, whatever that may be."

After shaking hands with Frank and Joe, Owens stepped out of the mission. Frank watched through a crumbling window as Owens walked quickly away. "I don't see anyone following him," Frank said.

"Good, but someone *is* following us," Joe said, standing at a window across the mission. Frank and Irene walked over to Joe. Standing in the shade of a distant tree was the redheaded man in the bomber jacket who had been taking pictures at Bandelier. He now appeared to be photographing the mission.

"He could have tailed us from Bandelier," Frank figured. "Or then again, he could still be a tourist. We should just ignore him for now."

"Okay, let's think," Joe said, moving restlessly through the empty mission. "If Weinhardt's breakthrough could enable the government to build a whole new breed of weapons, well, that's major. Could that be enough motivation for the government to kidnap Weinhardt and force him to complete his work?"

"I guess it's not impossible," Frank said, leaning against a stone wall. "But then how would they keep him from talking afterward?"

"They could kill him," Irene almost whispered.

"Do you really think the U.S. government would do that sort of thing?" Joe asked.

"There are governments inside governments," Irene said, glancing through the window at the man with the camera. "This whole thing could have been masterminded by a handful of extremists without other members of the government knowing about it. Some of these pro-military hawks are pretty scary."

"Weinhardt could also have been kidnapped by a private company," Frank said. "If they had the inside track on a superconductor that worked at close to room temperature, they could make billions off it."

"Not only did IDEA try to hire Weinhardt, according to Dean Patterson they were fairly aggressive about it," Joe said. "And they started right after the lexanium discovery."

"When we get back to the hotel," Frank said, "I'll surf the Net on my laptop and see what I can find on International Development Engineering Associates. There's bound to be something there."

As the trio drove back to Los Alamos, Frank wondered again about Weinhardt going underground willingly for the government, to make his breakthrough in total secrecy. Both Irene and the physicist at Lab 11 said Weinhardt was obsessed with his work. Frank didn't say anything, for fear of offending Irene, but he wasn't ruling out this scenario.

A few minutes before five, Joe parked the van right outside the Los Alamos gate. Shortly after, the Physics Club arrived, buzzing with excitement over the day's activities. Mr. Cribb took the wheel and began guiding the van back to the city of Santa Fe.

When the van returned to the hotel, Mr. Cribb instructed everyone to meet at the Purple Mesa restaurant at seven. Frank headed to his room to work at his computer, while Joe and Irene wandered into the Plaza.

As the sunset threw a gorgeous veil of pink and yellow over the adobe buildings surrounding the Plaza, Irene led Joe to the Palace of the Governors, a stately structure built by the Spanish in 1610. A long, shaded area in front of the building was crowded with Native Americans peddling arts and crafts made in their villages.

"I should buy something for Mom," Joe said, admiring a variety of silver and turquoise jewelry laid out on multicolored blankets. Joe spent several minutes carefully examining a collection of earrings. "Hey, Irene, which one of these do you think—"

Then Joe noticed Irene was no longer by his side. He glanced at all the nearby vendors but didn't see her. Joe scanned the Plaza behind him, which was crowded with people coming and going in all directions.

Finally Joe spotted Irene being dragged past the obelisk by somebody. He couldn't see who the kidnapper was, but the fear on Irene's face and the fact that she wasn't yelling told him there was a weapon at her back.

Chapter

7

As HE HUSTLED HIS WAY through the throng of people in the Plaza, Joe kept his eyes on Irene. When he noticed the person with her was wearing a gray cowboy hat, he realized it was Tom Condor. The man seemed to have something at Irene's back.

Joe broke into a sprint when he saw Condor and Irene disappear around the side of an adobe office building at one edge of the Plaza. Reaching the side of the building, Joe stopped, breathing hard. Condor and Irene were standing in a narrow passageway between two adobe walls. There was no one else around, and Condor had Irene pinned against one wall, a knife in his hand. Condor glared at Joe.

"How did you find us?" Joe demanded of Condor.

"I'm an Injun," Condor said sarcastically. "Remember, we're good at tracking." Condor's face was shadowed by the brim of his cowboy hat, but Joe could see the man was mad.

"What do you want?" Irene asked.

"Information," Condor answered.

"About what?" Joe said.

"When I left Bandelier this afternoon," Condor explained, "I thought I saw someone following me. Then I spent a few hours in a town near my pueblo. Well, everywhere I went, this guy was right behind me. He even followed me back to San Ildefonso. Scared my little girl half to death. I was thrown in jail once for my protesting, and she thought they had come to take me back. Anyway, I figured this guy had something to do with you kids, so I've come to get some answers."

"What did the guy look like?" Irene asked.

"He wore a bomber jacket," Condor replied.

"Red hair?" Joe asked.

"No, black," Condor answered.

Condor could have been lying, but Joe didn't think he was. "A man in a bomber jacket has been following us, too," Joe said. "I don't know who he is, but he might be connected to these two other guys with glasses who have also been following us. But then, for all I know, those two other guys with glasses might be working for you."

"You still think I might have murdered Weinhardt, don't you?" Condor said, angrily raising his voice.

"Forgive me, Mr. Condor," Irene spoke up, "but you do seem to have a pretty large chip on your shoulder. Not to mention a knife in your hand."

Joe watched the smoldering in Condor's eyes gradually die down. After a moment, Condor released Irene and put his knife away. Then he looked up at the sky and took a deep breath. When he finally spoke it was quietly, gently, as if he were a different person. "Ever since that digging at Bandelier," Condor confessed, "I haven't been myself. I had no right to scare you like that. But I have to watch my back."

"If you've done nothing wrong," Joe explained, "then that guy was probably just following you because he saw you with us."

"In other words," Condor said, "I just got mixed up in your little game of hide-and-seek."

"Maybe so," Joe admitted. "If that's the case, I'm sorry."

Condor nodded, accepting Joe's apology. "And I'm sorry I threatened both of you today," Condor said. "Tonight I'm going to the kiva. Hopefully I can cleanse some of this anger from my spirit. That is, if Mr. Trenchcoat doesn't follow me in there, too. Okay, Joe, Irene, take real good care of yourselves." Condor tipped his cowboy hat and headed out of the passageway.

"I think he's innocent," Joe told Irene. "It's mostly just a hunch, but it's a pretty strong one."

As Joe and Irene returned to the Plaza, the sunset was deepening, casting a lustrous red and violet glow across the adobe buildings. Joe noticed most of the Native American vendors at the Palace of Governors were packing up their wares for the day. The air was turning cooler, and Irene slipped her arm inside of Joe's for warmth.

As they headed for La Porta, Frank came running up to them. "I just downloaded some information on IDEA," Frank said, pulling a sheaf of papers from his jacket. "Their headquarters are in Switzerland, but the company also conducts research all over the world: the African desert, the South American rain forest, even Antarctica."

"Did you find anything that might hint at criminal activity?" Irene asked.

"No," Frank replied. "According to my information, they're completely legit. That doesn't mean there isn't more to the story, though. I left a message for Dad to see what he can find. I figured he could use his connections to access the FBI and Interpol files."

"Our dad is also a private detective," Joe informed Irene. "One of the best."

"Like father, like sons," Irene remarked.

Joe's eyes wandered to the other side of the Plaza, where he noticed Tom Condor stepping out of a toy store, carrying a plastic bag. Joe figured Condor had purchased something for his daughter.

Suddenly Joe spotted the red-haired man in the bomber jacket, and he could see the redhead was now following Condor. Though he knew it wasn't a wise move, Joe decided to run a little interference for Condor so the man could return to his pueblo in peace.

"I'll be right back," Joe said. "I'm going to help Condor."

"Condor?" Frank said, puzzled. "Joe, what are—"

But Joe was already trotting across the Plaza. Then Frank noticed Tom Condor and the red-haired man moving through the crowd in the distance. "What did I miss?" Frank asked Irene, keeping an eye on Joe.

"We just had a talk with Condor," Irene explained. "Now Joe thinks he's innocent, but a man in a bomber jacket has been following him, too. And I have no idea why Joe just ran off."

"He always does things without asking me," Frank said, shaking his head. "Come on." Frank and Irene began hurrying through the Plaza in pursuit of Joe.

Still trotting, Joe was moving past a collection of fancy arts-and-crafts shops. Just ahead, he saw the man in the bomber jacket and a little farther ahead, Tom Condor, who was still unaware he was being followed.

"Hey, how're you doing?" Joe said, catching

up to the red-haired man and walking alongside him.

"I'm fine," the man replied, not stopping, his eyes focused on Condor.

"Do you mind if I ask you a question?" Joe said, keeping pace with the man.

"Back off," the man snapped, shoving Joe away with his left hand.

"Why?" Joe said, grabbing the man's arm and forcing him to stop. "So you can follow that man, who doesn't have anything to do with any of this?"

"Let go of me, kid!" the man snarled, trying to free his arm.

"In a second," Joe replied, holding the arm tightly, not letting the man get away.

"Now!" the man ordered as he reached inside his jacket with his right hand. The next thing Joe knew, he was face-to-face with the barrel of a Beretta automatic pistol.

Joe instantly released the man's arm and backed away, the gun following his every move. But then Joe saw a swift flash of blue, which he realized was a leg in blue jeans, and a shoe clipping the barrel of the Beretta. The gun tumbled to the pavement.

"I don't like people pulling guns on my brother," Frank said, after he landed from his judo kick.

The man stooped for the gun, but Joe kicked it away as if it were a soccer ball. The gun skittered into the path of a large group of tourists passing by. The redhead went for his weapon, barreling through the crowd.

The second the group cleared out of the way, Frank dove for the man as if it were a football game and he had the ball.

The redhead got his hands on the weapon, but suddenly a foot came crashing down onto his wrist. "Acch!" the man cried in pain. Joe saw Irene standing over the redhead, digging the heel of her shoe into the man's arm.

"It's mine," Irene said, reaching down and yanking the pistol away from the man.

As Joe got up, he noticed several people slowing down to look at the commotion. "She's got a gun!" a man suddenly yelled. Then a woman screamed, and people began moving hurriedly away.

"Get up," Irene told the redhead as she pointed the Beretta at him, ignoring the frightened people around her. She was trying to play cool, but Joe noticed her hand was trembling.

"Freeze!" came a voice from somewhere above.

Frank whipped around and saw a second man in a bomber jacket standing on the roof of a one-story shop directly behind them. With both hands, steady as a practiced professional, the man was holding another pistol, and it was aimed directly at Irene.

Glued in place, both Hardy brothers slowly

raised their hands over their heads. But Irene kept her pistol trained on the redheaded man.

"Put down the gun!" the man on the roof called.

The immediate area was now in a state of chaos, some people fleeing the scene, others hovering at a safe distance to watch the sudden outbreak of action. Irene stubbornly kept the gun aimed at the redhead.

"Irene, put it down," Frank urged.

"No," Irene said, her voice and hand both trembling now. "I've been jerked around enough. Until I find my father, I'm not backing down from anybody!"

"Please, Irene," Joe whispered.

Frank saw the man on the roof shut one eye to improve his aim. The man's finger was on the trigger, and Frank knew Irene Weinhardt could be seriously injured, if not killed, in less than a second.

Chapter

8

"IF YOU'RE DEAD," Frank said urgently to Irene, "you won't be any help to your father at all. Put the gun down. Right now!"

This registered with Irene. She slowly set the gun on the ground, then lifted her hands in the air.

As Frank breathed a sigh of relief, the red-haired man snatched up the gun and stuffed it in his coat. "Special Agent Abrams of the FBI," the redhead said as he flipped open his wallet to show them his badge. While he began frisking Frank, Joe, and Irene with experienced hands, Frank watched the other man climb nimbly down from the roof.

"It's all right, folks," Abrams called to the gathered crowd when he was finished with the gun check. "Just a little mix-up, that's all. Let's keep it moving." Some of the bystanders began moving on while others stuck around to gape.

As the man from the roof approached, Frank saw it was Special Agent Martinez, the FBI agent who had interrogated him that morning. "Hello again," Martinez said, his black hair still perfectly in place. "Why don't we play it casual and take a walk?"

"Let's arrest them," Abrams urged. "The lady pulled a gun on a federal agent, for crying out loud!" Martinez waved for Abrams to pipe down.

"What's going on?" Joe asked as the two federal agents began walking through the Plaza with Irene and the Hardys.

"After I heard Frank's story this morning," Martinez said, "I checked our files on Weinhardt. Everything said the guy died in a car accident. But the whole thing seemed a little funny to me, so I got Abrams to put a tail on you three, just to see what you were up to. After he reported to me that you were talking to Tom Condor, I picked up Condor's tail myself. We've already got a thick file on him for his activism."

"So you were the black-haired man following Condor," Irene said.

"Right," Martinez confirmed. "But just now Abrams and I were planning to switch targets. That's why Abrams here started following Condor. Then you guys stumbled into the way. Obviously you have been busy this afternoon. Why don't you fill me in?"

Once again, Frank figured he had better tell the truth. As the group strolled around the Plaza, Frank related everything that had happened since they had left Los Alamos. When he was done, the group wandered into the center of the Plaza.

"All right," Martinez said, resting a highly polished shoe on a bench. "It does appear something funny is going on here—funny and dangerous. I doubt Tom Condor is involved, but those fellows in the glasses certainly are. I'm going to suggest to my superiors that we make the Weinhardt disappearance a top-priority case."

"I should hope so," Irene said emphatically.

"How can we help?" Joe asked.

"By doing nothing," Martinez replied sternly. "You've convinced me there's foul play here, and I'll get right to work on it. But listen, those guys with glasses are probably killers, and I don't want any of you hurt. Stay with the Physics Club every minute from now on and leave the detective work to the FBI. I know how to find you, and I'll keep you posted when the time is right. Do you read me?"

"Yes, we read you," Irene answered.

"I still say we should arrest them," Abrams muttered.

"You're probably right," Martinez said, his eyes meeting Frank, then Joe, then Irene. "But I'm not going to. Because I *know* these kids are going to lay off now. All right, *amigos, buenas noches.*"

Martinez clapped Abrams on the shoulder, and the two FBI agents walked swiftly away from the Plaza.

"I read him, but I don't want to lay off," Irene said, putting her hands in her coat pockets. "The FBI hasn't done very well on this case so far, and I don't trust them to do any better."

"There's another reason we shouldn't lay off," Joe mentioned. "If some government mavericks are involved in your dad's disappearance, Martinez could know about it by now. Maybe they brought him in on it. Maybe he wants us off the case for reasons other than our own safety."

"That's a definite possibility," Irene said.

"It's almost seven," Frank said. "We've got to meet the Physics Club at the Purple Mesa restaurant. Might as well continue this over a nice meal."

By the time Irene and the Hardys left the Plaza, the city was cloaked in darkness. Aided by the glow from the iron street lamps, Frank kept an eye on the people passing by, on their way home or to a hotel or to a nearby eatery.

As Frank pulled up his jacket collar, the group turned onto a less busy street. Though he wasn't aware of footsteps, Frank soon had the unmistakable feeling that he, Joe, and Irene were being followed.

Frank remembered the warning on the cliff:

"Be out of town by nightfall—or else." He expected the men with glasses to materialize at any moment. Instead of only trying to scare Irene and the Hardys, chances were that this time the men would be trying to assassinate them.

As Joe and Irene stepped into the Purple Mesa restaurant, Frank glanced back and spotted the men in glasses, lingering in a nearby doorway.

Inside the candle-lit restaurant, Mr. Cribb and the rest of the Physics club were seated at several tables. Many of the students had shopping bags filled with souvenirs they'd purchased before dinner. After greeting the group, and receiving an arched eyebrow from Mr. Cribb, Frank, Joe, and Irene sat at a table by themselves.

"I got a glimpse of our friends near the door," Frank told Joe and Irene. "They'll probably dog us everywhere now. I think they mean to kill us. But they're pros. They'll wait for a moment when there're absolutely no witnesses. I'm thinking from now on maybe Irene should—"

"No way, Frank," Irene broke in. "I know what you're about to say and you can just forget it. The three of us are a team, every step of the way. Got it?"

Frank and Joe both nodded, each looking at Irene with admiration.

"Now, listen," Irene said, her hazel eyes flashing. "We might be able to turn this situation to our advantage. We don't know who's responsible for my father's disappearance, but we do know

69

those guys with glasses are connected to the source, be it Condor, someone in the government, IDEA, or some other company. They're probably just goons hired to get us out of the way, but if we can discover something about them—where they go, whom they contact—we might have a trail to follow."

"Good point," Frank said. "The trick is, to do it without them killing us first."

Suddenly Joe's eyes landed on Ed Questal, who was engaged in an intense technological debate with Tiny Marvelson at the neighboring table. "Hey, Ed," Joe called, "have you finished that little gadget?"

"I sure have," Ed called back proudly. "It works unbelievably well!"

A sly smile formed on Joe's lips. "I've got a plan," he said to Frank and Irene. "We'll have to bring in Ed and Tiny, but I think it's crazy enough to work."

"I'm nervous already," Frank said. "Spill it."

"You and Irene leave the restaurant early," Joe explained. "One or both of those guys will follow. Then Ed, Tiny, and I will slip out through the kitchen. You lead the party on your tail to a designated place, where my team and I will be waiting. We cause a diversion that allows us to slip Ed's transmitting device on the party following you. The diversion also allows you guys to get away. Then we follow the guy wearing Ed's device without him knowing we're on him.

With a little luck, he'll lead us to something of interest."

"It's risky," Frank warned.

"Not if it's well planned," Irene countered.

After the waitress took their orders, Frank, Joe, and Irene gathered around a map of downtown Santa Fe and began planning the operation.

Forty minutes later, after a light supper, Frank and Irene stepped out of the restaurant and began walking down the street. By the light of the street lamps, Frank saw a few other people strolling by. Witnesses, Frank thought. Glancing back, Frank glimpsed the two men with glasses. "They're both on us," Frank whispered to Irene. "That makes things even easier."

Soon Frank and Irene turned onto another street, passing shops and restaurants. This block, too, had potential witnesses. Frank reviewed the charted path in his mind, which was a circuitous route that would soon lead them into the second part of the plan.

Ten minutes later, Joe, Ed, and Tiny were standing beneath the awning of a restaurant on Water Street. Each boy was now wearing a loudly colored poncho and a sombrero, souvenirs purchased by members of the Physics Club. The disguises weren't brilliant, but Joe figured they were sufficient.

"Here they come," Joe said as he watched

71

Frank and Irene stroll into view on the sidewalk across the street. Several yards behind them, Joe saw the two men with glasses, keeping perfect pace with their prey.

"Okay, guys," Joe told Ed and Tiny. "Lights, camera, action."

At once, the three boys started joking and laughing like three teenagers having a boisterous night out in Santa Fe. The trio crossed the street, heading for the sidewalk where Frank and Irene were walking, shadowed by the two men.

As soon as Frank and Irene passed by, Tiny gave Joe a good-natured roughhouse shove, and Joe went slamming into the man in the gray sweatjacket.

The man grunted as he stumbled backward, but he didn't seem to recognize Joe.

"Hey what's the big idea?" Joe yelled to Tiny.

"You tell me!" Tiny yelled back.

"Okay, I will," Joe responded. Then he gave Tiny a good hard shove straight into the man in the blue sweatjacket, who reeled a few steps. As the man in blue struggled to keep his balance, Joe saw Ed slip the transmitting device into the shoulder bag the man was wearing.

"Come on, cool it, guys!" Ed yelled at his friends. "You almost knocked these two down!"

The men in sweatjackets started after Frank and Irene, but Tiny and Joe stood in their way, blocking their path and their view. "Hey, we're really sorry," Tiny said to the two men. "By the way, nice glasses. Is this some sort of retro look?"

"Yeah, I'm sorry, too," Joe said, disguising his voice. "Don't mind us."

"These clowns are way out of hand," Ed said, also stepping in front of the men. "I think we're all having a bit too much fun tonight."

The two men angrily shoved past the teenagers, then glanced up the street for Frank and Irene. But they didn't see their target. After a few whispered words, they trotted off in opposite directions.

Joe knew Frank and Irene had made a quick turn onto another street while the goons were being distracted. He also knew they would be following another circuitous path that would make it almost impossible for the goons to find them.

"See if it's working," Joe told Ed.

Ed pulled out a small plastic box, pushed a button, and a steady beeping sounded. "As long as we stay within fourteen hundred feet, this beep will keep us tuned in to Mr. Blue's whereabouts," Ed explained. "If the beep gets stronger, we're closer. If it gets fainter, we're farther away."

"Ah, the miracles of science!" Joe said. "Let's go."

As planned, Frank and Irene had zigged and zagged a few times and had just turned onto yet another street. The men in sweatjackets were nowhere to be seen. Two couples strolled by, one chatting, the other looking inside darkened shop windows, and nearby Frank heard the mellow tones of a church bell tolling the hour.

"The plan came off great," Frank told Irene. "We'll just lie low while the others do their work."

Frank and Irene turned onto another street, one that was completely deserted. The only sounds Frank heard were the soft thumps of his and Irene's footsteps on the pavement.

Suddenly Frank was aware of another pair of footsteps. They were coming from hard-soled shoes that made distinctive clicks on the sidewalk. He knew these footsteps didn't belong to either of the men with glasses as they both wore rubber-soled shoes.

Even so, something about the steps bothered Frank. They were staying perfectly in rhythm with the steps he and Irene were taking. Frank wondered if they were being trailed by one of the FBI men, knowing the special agents favored suits and dress shoes. No, Frank told himself, the person following them wanted them to know they were being followed.

Was there another man—a third man—working with the two men in glasses?

A Spanish mission loomed in the darkness up ahead. "Come on," Frank said as he quickly led Irene onto the grassy lawn surrounding the mission. After pushing Irene into a protective niche where two of the mission's adobe walls came together, Frank glanced at the sidewalk.

A figure stood only a few yards away. Frank could make out a man wearing a black sweatshirt with the hood up and glasses with thick black frames. The man's right hand hung at his side, and Frank could see he was holding a gun. Frank glanced up and down the street. There was no one in the vicinity.

"You were told to be out of town by nightfall," the figure spoke in a low voice. "And still you are playing games. But you lose. It is time to die."

Frank shoved Irene to the ground and fell on top of her. At the same time, a gunshot rang out.

Chapter

9

FRANK HEARD A BULLET bite into the adobe wall directly above his body. He realized the bullet was fired from a semiautomatic gun with a suppressor device. It fired one muted shot at a time. It was a perfect instrument for hits, but it did allow a very brief grace period between bullets.

Staying on top of Irene, Frank craned his head away from the wall. He saw there was a side door in the mission, about ten feet away. The door was indented into the wall, protected on either side by a foot of adobe. "There's a door up ahead," Frank whispered. "Let's run for it. Now!"

Frank and Irene sprang up and darted for the door, Frank pressing a hand on Irene's back to keep her bent over. As they ran, Frank heard another shot from the gun. When they reached the door, Frank shoved Irene into the area protected by the adobe. As expected, the door was locked.

"Hello!" Frank called, banging on the wooden door. "Open up, please! It's an emergency!" Frank heard another shot. A chunk of adobe flew off the wall, and Irene let out a terrified gasp.

Frank continued banging, but no one answered the door. Though he could pick locks and even had a pick in his pocket, he knew it would take at least a minute. He didn't have that much time.

"Someone rang that church bell only a few minutes ago," Frank said, still banging on the door. "Whoever it was must be in here!"

"The guy with a gun," Irene whispered nervously. "He's on the lawn. I see him!"

"Scream," Frank instructed.

Irene let out a bloodcurdling scream.

"Open up!" Frank called, pounding loudly on the door. "Please! It's an emergency!"

Another shot. Another chunk of adobe flew off the wall, inches from Frank's head.

Irene stopped screaming. Frank turned to see if she had been hit. "Frank, look," Irene said, pointing.

Frank turned, seeing a beam of light slice through the darkened street. It was a car, a witness. Even better, a rectangular light on the roof indicated it was a taxi.

"Come on!" Frank said, grabbing Irene by the

wrist. They dashed across the grassy lawn straight into the middle of the street, waving their hands and yelling, "Taxi, taxi!"

The taxi screeched to a stop in front of them. Frank and Irene opened the back door and hurried inside. "La Porta, please," Frank told the driver as he slammed the door shut.

The taxi accelerated away.

"Oh, that was scary," Irene said, holding her chest and leaning against Frank. "I don't know if my heart will ever stop pounding!"

As soon as they reached the hotel, Frank and Irene went to Frank's room on the fourth floor. Joe was not there, but an E-mail letter from Fenton Hardy had been sent to Frank's laptop. Frank printed the letter, then read it as he and Irene descended the stairs back to the lobby.

They sat on a leather couch to wait for the return of Joe, Ed, and Tiny. No visitors were in the lobby, but there was a man at the front desk. Irene checked her watch several times while Frank finished the letter.

"Anything significant?" Irene asked.

"Possibly," Frank said. "Apparently the most important player for IDEA is the man who heads up their research-and-development department. His name is Jonathan Pless. The guy has a reputation for always being on top on the latest scientific and technological breakthroughs. But according to Interpol's files, his methods are somewhat dubious."

"How do you mean?" Irene asked.

"Though nothing has ever been proven," Frank explained, "Interpol believes that Pless gets a lot of his information through espionage. They also suspect he once had a scientist murdered so he could steal the patent on an important drug the scientist had formulated. The files say Pless will stop at absolutely nothing to bring the latest and most lucrative ideas to his company."

"He could have had spies at Los Alamos," Irene speculated. "Pless finds out my dad is closing in on the superconductor breakthrough and tries to hire him. When he sees my dad isn't for sale, he has him kidnapped. It's crazy, but it fits the profile."

Just then Frank was surprised to see Joe come bounding down a set of stairs and across the lobby. "Where have you been, gringo?" Frank asked as Joe approached, no longer wearing the poncho and sombrero.

Joe flopped on the couch and said, "Ed's little device worked to perfection. We followed Mr. Blue. He spent some time looking for you guys, then met up with Mr. Gray, and they returned to their hotel together. And their hotel happens to be . . ."

"Don't tell me they're staying right here," Irene said, gripping Joe's shoulder.

"Two floors below us," Joe announced. "Rooms 203 and 209. They're in them right now.

We should have a look in their rooms as soon as they're out. I sent Ed and Tiny back to their own rooms. They still don't know the real story, but let's keep it that way, all right? So, how did things go for you guys?"

"Not great," Frank replied. "It turns out there's a third man after us. He picked up our trail and would have iced us if it weren't for a very well-timed taxi. But I did get some interesting information from Dad." Frank handed Joe the letter from their father.

"A third man," Joe said, taking the letter. "Hmmm."

"What are you thinking?" Frank asked.

"Chances are he's also staying here," Joe said. "If he's not back yet, we could check his room now."

"But how do we get his room number without knowing his name," Frank wondered. "Maybe if we—"

"Leave it to me," Irene said, whipping off her glasses. "You know, there are certain advantages to having a girl on the team."

Irene rose from the couch and sauntered over to the stout middle-aged man behind the check-in desk. With some amusement, Frank and Joe watched Irene smile, shake her hair a few times, laugh, and finally ask a series of questions. The man seemed to be answering all of them in an exceptionally friendly manner. A few moments later, Irene sauntered back to Frank and Joe.

"The third man is staying in Room 213," Irene said, returning the glasses to her face. "And, no, the clerk doesn't think he's back yet. How did I do?"

"First-class flirtation," Joe said with a wink.

"That staircase Joe just used is the only way to the second floor of the north wing," Frank said. "You two keep an eye on it. If you see anyone climb it who even might be the third man, call the room. I'll answer, but you speak first."

Minutes later Frank was walking down a carpeted hallway toward Room 213. When he reached the door, Frank knocked and waited. No answer. Frank pulled a metal pick from his pocket and inserted it into the door's cylinder.

Very quietly, Frank opened the door. He listened a moment for the sound of someone breathing in the darkened room, then he switched on a light. The room, also decorated with a Southwestern flavor, looked as though it could have been occupied by any average businessman or tourist.

The bed was still made, there was a pair of pants draped over a chair, and there was a laptop computer on the desk alongside a magazine, a newspaper, and a pack of chewing gum.

Frank checked the laptop for an alarm system or even a tiny sliver of tape or a hair left as a signal that it had been tampered with. Finding nothing, Frank opened the laptop and turned it on. As expected, the files were locked. Knowing it could take a while to slip past the password, he decided to leave the computer for later.

Frank searched the desk, the pants pockets, and the rest of the room, finding nothing. He leafed through a magazine, stopping at the subscription card inside. On the line marked Address, the word *Alaska* was written in ink. Probably nothing.

Frank looked in the bathroom and found a suitcase. Very slowly, he began moving the zipper across the metal grooves that ran around the perimeter of the suitcase. Frank's heart stopped when a bell jingled. Was it an alarm? No, it was just the telephone.

He walked over to the phone on the desk, figuring it would be Joe telling him the third man was on the way up. But before Frank reached the phone, he heard a high-pitched beeping sound, which he realized was the modem on the laptop. A message was coming in. Taking a seat at the desk, Frank opened the laptop. The beeping stopped, but a window appeared on the upper half of the laptop's screen that said, "Receiving incoming message." Frank tapped a few keys, but a window appeared on the lower half of the screen that asked, "What is your password?"

Almost without thinking, Frank felt his fingers typing the word *Alaska.*

A message appeared on the upper half of the

screen. It read, "Orion, are you home? It's Cosmo."

Frank smiled, pleased at his luck, and typed, "Yes, Orion is here." The words appeared on the lower window, then Frank pressed the Return key to send the message.

Seconds later another message appeared on the upper window. It read, "How are the brats? Have they responded to threats or are they still pursuing W?"

If W is Weinhardt, Frank thought, it's awfully nice of them not to disguise his name any better. He typed in: "The brats seem to have backed off for now. Will keep a close eye on them." Again Frank pressed Return to send the message.

The following message was transmitted back, "Good. Anything else to report?"

Frank was not ready to sign off so quickly. He sent the following message: "Not at this end. How is W getting along?"

This message returned: "Seems depressed. Complains of headaches a lot. Eye strain, too."

Frank was guessing W meant Weinhardt, but he wanted to make sure. He thought a moment, then sent the following message: "Typical physicist!"

This message returned: "Exactly!"

Bingo, Frank thought. A physicist named W pretty much had to be Weinhardt. And this meant Weinhardt was alive. But where was he?

Frank sent the message: "How is the weather?"

This message returned: "Not too bad. It's been holding around zero lately but should start getting much colder soon."

That's interesting, Frank thought. Obviously Cosmo is in the same location as Weinhardt, and it's zero degrees there. But where in the world are they?

Frank decided to sprinkle in some innocent small talk before asking another leading question. He sent the following message: "Hope you brought thick socks."

Meanwhile, in the lobby of the hotel, Joe was standing by a public telephone next to the hotel's darkened restaurant. He was hidden from most of the lobby but had a clear view of Irene, who was seated on the couch, reading a newspaper.

Twelve minutes had passed without event, during which Joe had read the letter sent by his father. But then Joe saw Irene crane her head as if to look at someone from behind the newspaper. Irene waited a moment, as if following somebody's movements, then pointed a finger directly at Joe.

This was the signal, Joe knew. The third man was on his way! Joe punched the numbers 213 on the telephone, waited, then heard a busy signal. Thinking he may have gotten a wrong number, he hung up and quickly punched the number again. Once more he received the sour tones of a busy signal.

Joe hurried into the lobby, seeing no one but Irene and the man at the check-in desk. "Is he on his way?" Joe asked urgently.

"He's already on the steps," Irene said. "Same black jacket, hood still up. Did you call?"

"The line was busy," Joe said, rushing for the stairwell. "Stay right here!"

Back in Room 213, Frank was still carrying on a pleasant on-line conversation with the unknown party who he now assumed was Orion's superior. Frank was almost chuckling at the ease of the deception.

Suddenly Frank stopped typing in midsentence. Were those footsteps in the hallway? He clenched his teeth, remembering that the computer modem would be tying up the phone line, which meant Joe would not be able to send the warning signal.

Then Frank heard the sound of a key turning in the door's cylinder.

As Frank turned around, the door swung wide open, and he saw the figure of a man in a black sweatjacket with the hood up. Frank couldn't make out the man's features, but he could clearly see the man's right hand.

The assassin held a pistol with a suppressor device attached to the barrel, and the gun was aimed directly at Frank's chest.

Chapter

10

FRANK LEAPED FOR THE FLOOR, turning the chair over to use it as a shield, just as a shot fired from the gun. As a sliver of wood flew off the chair, Frank scurried under the desk, pulling the chair in after him.

He was closed in on all sides, but his little shelter wouldn't last long. Across the room, Frank saw the black pants of the gunman approaching. . . .

But suddenly the gunman grunted, and Frank saw a pair of blue jeans right next to the black pants. When Frank eased out the chair, he saw Joe behind the attacker, using both hands to grip the gunman's weapon hand.

Frank hurried out from under the desk. The gun pointed and fired. He flew against the wall, dodging the wild shot.

The gunman back-ended his elbow into Joe's stomach, causing Joe to let go, the wind knocked out of his lungs. Before the gunman could swing the gun to Joe, Frank was on him, gripping the man's right wrist, struggling to keep the gun away from his brother.

Suddenly the gunman jerked the gun upward, crashing it into Frank's face, right between the eyes. Everything turned to pain and blackness.

Seeing that Frank was down, Joe dove behind the bed and crawled underneath it. As he lay on the floor, he saw the gunman's black pants approaching the bed.

Then Joe heard a loud hissing sound and saw the gunman stagger. After crawling out from under the bed on the opposite side, he saw Irene spraying white foam from a fire extinguisher into the gunman's face. Covering his face with his left arm, still clutching the gun with his right hand, the gunman backed away from the fire extinguisher.

"Where's my father?" Irene screamed, staying beside the bed.

Joe saw Frank was leaning against a wall, dazed, and the gunman was now by the door, his face and upper body plastered with the white chemical foam.

Irene heaved the fire extinguisher at the gunman, catching his right arm, and the pistol fell to the floor. Joe started for it.

But the gunman ripped off his glasses, which had protected his eyes from the foam, and Joe stopped, realizing the man would get the weapon first.

"Open the window!" Joe yelled to Irene as he ran for Frank.

"Crawl!" Joe yelled as he jerked his brother to the floor. A bullet zipped into the carpet, inches away. With Joe helping Frank, the two brothers scrambled madly across the floor toward the window, which Irene had pushed open.

A bullet ripped a lamp shade near the window. "Out!" Joe yelled at Irene, who quickly climbed outside, Frank and Joe following.

They were standing on an adobe ledge one story above the hotel's back courtyard. "Bend your knees, Irene," Joe called. "Frank, can you jump?"

Frank nodded as the windowpane exploded from a gunshot. "Go!" Joe shouted.

Frank, Irene, and Joe jumped from the ledge, everyone making a safe landing on the pavement below.

"Run," Joe yelled, grabbing hold of Frank, who held on to Irene. The trio went tearing past the groomed shrubbery and garden statues of the courtyard.

"Is he following us?" Irene called as she ran.

"I don't think so," Joe said, glancing back. "He's probably going for the other two guys."

"Where to?" Irene panted.

"The parking lot," Joe called. "We can hot-wire the van and take off." Joe opened the courtyard's wrought-iron gate, and they made a dash for the lot behind the hotel.

Frank was alert by the time they got to the van. "Stand back," he warned. As Joe and Irene kept their distance, Frank spun around, then sent his right foot straight into the van's driver-side window. The glass shattered on impact.

Frank opened the door, swept away pieces of glass with his sleeve, then pulled a knob that released the van's front hood. "Get in," Frank told Irene. "Careful of the glass."

Irene scurried onto the front seat. Frank stood watch while Joe tampered with the network of wires under the hood. Within moments, the vehicle's engine sprang to life, and both Hardys climbed into the van. Joe shifted gears, then sent the van hurtling out of the parking lot and onto the street.

"Let's go somewhere on the other side of town," Joe suggested. "Preferably a place where there's plenty of people around. Irene, tell me where."

"Oh, there's so many fun things to do in Santa Fe," Irene quipped. "It's a tourist's dream."

"Irene, listen to me," Frank said, touching his throbbing forehead where he'd been smashed by the gun. "Your father is alive!"

89

As Joe drove, Frank explained everything he had just learned in Room 213. Twenty minutes later Joe parked the van in the street somewhere on the western edge of the city. The Hardys and Irene walked several blocks, finally coming to a cafe. Inside, the place was dark and crowded, which made it perfect as a temporary safe haven.

Frank, Joe, and Irene took a seat near the back, from which they could watch the door. When a waitress came, they ordered soft drinks and an order of Southwestern appetizers.

"Okay," Joe said over the din of the crowd, "let's evaluate what Frank discovered in Room 213."

"Cosmo said the temperature wherever he was is currently around zero degrees," Frank said, keeping an eye on the door. "He also said it will be getting much colder soon."

"It's March now," Joe pointed out. "If the temperature is getting colder, they must be in the southern hemisphere."

"There's a circle that runs around the bottom of the globe known as the Convergence," Irene said, her finger drawing a circle on the table. "The only part of the southern hemisphere that gets significantly colder than zero is inside the Convergence. And there's only one country there, Antarctica."

"Antarctica?" Joe exclaimed. "Why would your father be in Antarctica?"

As the waitress arrived with the soft drinks and

appetizers, Frank pulled some papers from his coat pocket and began leafing through them.

"Antarctica has many unique features that make it useful for scientific research," Irene explained. "In fact, that's mostly what goes on down there."

"But would any of those features be useful for your father's work," Joe asked, reaching for an appetizer.

"Yes!" Irene cried, slapping the table with a sudden realization. "The magnetic conditions in Antarctica are different from everywhere else in the world. That's why compasses don't work there. Magnetism is related to electricity, which is related to superconductivity. Which means there could be a significant reason Antarctica is a good place for my father to continue his research!"

"Well," Joe said, chewing his food, "that's probably where he is then."

"And listen," Frank said, lifting his eyes from the papers. "This is the information I downloaded on IDEA. Among other places, I remembered reading that they're conducting research in Antarctica. I just double-checked and I was right."

"But they can't be," Irene said, after a sip of her soft drink. "An international treaty declares that Antarctica is to be used only for nonprofit scientific study. Numerous countries are allowed to have bases there, but absolutely no private business is allowed."

"Maybe they found a way around that," Frank said, glancing at the top paper. "The actual wording here is 'IDEA is contributing money to be used for research at the Russian base of Voboskov.' On the surface, everything seems to be legal, but who knows what's going on underneath?"

"Nine-tenths of an iceberg is underwater," Joe mentioned. "I'd say there's an excellent chance this Jonathan Pless character Dad told us about is the one who kidnapped Kenneth Weinhardt. Maybe it's time we go to the feds."

"No," Irene argued. "The U.S. government has plenty of research bases in Antarctica, and I think there's still a chance my dad is being held prisoner at one of those. We have to keep this information to ourselves until we know for sure no one in the government is a part of it."

"I guess the best thing to do," Frank said, "would be to go to this Voboskov station and see if Weinhardt is there. If he is, we know IDEA is responsible. If he's not, we keep searching for him."

"And we should leave soon," Joe added. "Tonight if possible. It's only a matter of time before those goons catch up with us and kill us."

"Whoa, slow down," Irene said, touching Joe's arm. "It's not all that easy getting to Antarctica. It's not exactly the Bahamas, you know."

"Excuse me," a man said, suddenly leaning

over Irene's shoulder. "May I join you a moment?"

The man appeared to be in his mid-thirties, a well-built frame visible beneath his maroon sweater. He was ruggedly handsome, with dark curly hair, and Joe noticed he spoke with a Hispanic accent.

"Actually we're having a private conversation," Frank said, wondering if the guy was simply nosy or potentially dangerous.

"I see," the man said politely. "It's just that I thought I heard you say you were going to Antarctica tonight and I found that very interesting."

"Why?" Joe asked.

"Because, as it turns out, I am also going to Antarctica tonight," the man replied.

"Oh, really?" Joe said, feeling sure this was a setup of some kind.

"Yes, I am," the man said, pulling up a chair beside Irene. "You see, I am a geophysicist working at the University of New Mexico. I go to Antarctica periodically for research."

"What kind of research?" Irene asked.

"Mostly underground magnetism," the man said. "By the way, my name is Antonio Salvador."

"Where are you from?" Frank asked.

"Argentina," Salvador answered. "In fact, I am going to an Argentine base in Antarctica."

"This is quite a coincidence," Irene observed.

"Not so much," Salvador said with a grin. "You see, there are many scientific people in

New Mexico, and in Antarctica it is pretty much only scientists—meteorologists, physicists, oceanographers, and, of course, geophysicists like me. So, you see, it's not that big of a coincidence. Perhaps just a small one."

"Well, okay," Joe said with a shrug. "You're going to Antarctica. Have a nice trip."

"I'm sure I will," Salvador said, not taking the hint to leave. "But if you folks are also going to Antarctica tonight, perhaps we could arrange to take the same flights. It's such a long journey, and I would love to have some company on the way."

Frank studied the overly friendly Argentine a moment. He could be part of a trap or his story could be completely true. Frank knew if they were going to Antarctica, they needed to do it soon. And they would also need some help getting around once they arrived. He decided to feel out the situation further.

"Maybe you could tell us a few things," Frank said. "Without going into details, we need to visit the Voboskov base. Do you know of it?"

"Yes," Salvador answered. "It's a small base belonging to the Russian government. It's about a hundred and fifty miles inland. How are you planning to get there?"

"We're still figuring that out," Frank said. "It's all, well . . . kind of complicated."

"I'll tell you what," Salvador said, helping himself to an appetizer. "If you travel with me, I will help you get to Voboskov. I'm catching a plane out of Albuquerque at one-thirty-five this morning. I can drive you to the airport, and I'm sure you can book the same flights I'm taking. Please, come along and I guarantee your safe arrival in Voboskov. You can trust Antonio Salvador."

Frank studied the charming smile on Salvador's face, wondering if it was true or false. The whole thing looks way too easy to be real, Frank decided.

"Antonio, we appreciate the offer," Frank said, "but I really don't think so. And I'm afraid we need to be going. All the same, it was great meeting you." Frank left some money on the table for the bill, then stood up to leave. Joe and Irene followed suit. "Well, I'd better be going, too," Salvador said, rising from his chair. "It's already eleven o'clock."

Salvador followed Irene and the Hardys out of the club and into the chilly night air. Then he insisted on walking with them. "So why is it you need to get to Voboskov?" Salvador asked Frank as the group headed for the van.

"Oh, it's a long story," Frank said.

"I don't like this guy," Irene whispered to Joe. "Either he's very lonely or he's hanging on to us for a reason."

"I hope he's just lonely," Joe whispered back.

When they got to the van, Frank opened the front door, noticing that Salvador was checking out the shattered side window. "Okay, Antonio," Frank said, offering a hand to the Argentine, "we really have to be going now. Have a great trip."

But instead of shaking Frank's hand, Salvador grabbed Frank by the shoulders and hurled him roughly onto the sidewalk.

FRANK SPRANG UP, readying himself for a fight.

"Everybody stand back!" Salvador cried.

Joe ploughed a shoulder into Salvador's chest, knocking him backward, but Salvador grabbed Joe and flung him away with surprising strength.

"I said stand back," Salvador called, moving away from the van. "There's a bomb in there! I smell nitro!"

Everyone froze a moment. Then Joe took a cautious step toward the van and saw a brightly colored piñata sitting on the front seat. "I don't remember that being there before," he said.

Salvador picked up an empty soda bottle from the sidewalk. After signaling the others to move way back, he tossed the bottle at the piñata. With a boom and a blinding flash of light, the piñata exploded, cracking the windshield and blowing out some of the front-seat upholstery.

"More fiesta fun from our friendly hit men," Irene remarked.

"I deal with explosives in my work," Salvador explained. "As soon as Frank opened the van door, I smelled nitroglycerine. It's a subtle odor but one well known to me."

"Good thing for me," Frank said. "That piñata would have blown the second I touched it."

"You see," Salvador said, breaking into a broad smile, "I told you I could be trusted. But now I am even more curious to know what you folks are up to."

Frank considered the Salvador situation very carefully. The Hardys needed to see if Weinhardt was at Voboskov, and they needed to do it before the men with glasses killed them. On top of that, they needed someone familiar with Antarctica to help them get there. Salvador's sudden appearance looked very suspicious, but the fact that the Argentine had just stopped them all from getting blown to smithereens made him seem a lot more believable. Trusting Salvador was a risk, to be sure, but Frank decided it was a risk that had a good chance of paying off.

"Okay, Salvador," Frank said, "we'll travel to Antarctica with you, and you'll get us to Voboskov."

"Safe and warm," Salvador said, giving Frank a hearty pat on the back. Salvador led Frank, Joe, and Irene to his car, which was parked nearby, and then the Argentine drove toward La Porta so Frank, Joe, and Irene could pick up their things. On the way, Joe gave Salvador an only partially true explanation of why they were going to Voboskov. He explained they needed to find Irene's father, a physicist. Salvador seemed to buy the story.

When the group arrived at the hotel's lobby, Salvador immediately went to make a phone call, giving Irene and the Hardys a moment alone in the deserted lobby.

"Irene, on the way over here I realized something," Frank said. "If the folks at Voboskov are the bad guys, chances are they'll have descriptions of me and Joe, if not computerized images. But they won't be expecting us, and if we comb our hair differently, dress differently, we have a shot of slipping in under some phony cover story. But you're Weinhardt's daughter. They're bound to have a better idea what you look like. I think you need to let Joe and me handle this alone."

"But—" Irene started to protest.

"He's right," Joe said. "Besides, I'll bet you don't have your passport with you."

"Do you?" Irene asked.

"Joe and I carry our passports everywhere," Frank said. "Unexpected trips seem to come up a lot."

Irene turned toward a window, silent for a moment. Frank was expecting a slug in the stomach any second, but when Irene turned back to the Hardys, she took a small photograph from her wallet. "This is a picture of my dad," Irene said, handing Joe the photo. "It will help you recognize him."

Frank and Joe both looked at the photo, which showed Weinhardt with his arms around his wife and Irene. The physicist had wild graying hair and a round face that made him seem as friendly as Santa Claus. Looks like a nice family, Joe thought.

After the Hardys fetched their bags upstairs, Frank, Joe, and Irene returned to the lobby. Still on the phone, Salvador waved, indicating he was almost finished. It was time for goodbyes with Irene.

"Obviously you can't tell anyone where we're going," Frank told Irene. "If our cover story is going to work, we need complete secrecy."

"I understand," Irene said, nodding.

"Another thing," Frank said. "From now on, I want you to stay with the Physics Club every second. And I mean *every single second*. As long as you're with a group of people, you should be okay."

"Yes, sir," Irene replied.

"And there's one more thing," Joe mentioned. "I'm afraid we're leaving you with the toughest job of all."

"What's that?" Irene asked.

"You have to tell Mr. Cribb about the van," Joe said with a grin.

"Goodbye, guys," Irene said, her hazel eyes glowing with gratitude. "Be real careful, and bring me a souvenir from down south."

"I hope it's your father," Frank replied.

Irene gave both Frank and Joe a hug. Frank very much hoped he would see Irene Weinhardt again, and Joe was even thinking he might like to date her—if he made it back from the trip alive.

Due to the late hour, the Albuquerque airport was practically empty. Salvador picked up his tickets, and Frank and Joe, using a credit card, were able to purchase tickets on the same flights Salvador had booked. The flight itinerary was Albuquerque to Dallas to Brazil to Chile, then finally on to Antarctica.

"Once we get to Antarctica," Salvador explained, "we will take a helicopter to Voboskov and land there, pretending we need to make some repairs. I'm sure we'll be invited inside the base. No one turns away a guest in Antarctica. Then it shouldn't be too hard for you to see if this physicist is at the base."

"We'll say we're grad students assisting you," Frank added.

Soon Frank, Joe, and Salvador were on a 727 bound for Dallas, Texas. Frank settled into his seat, knowing it was going to a very long time before they got to Voboskov. Shutting his eyes, he tried to keep his mind from dwelling on how cold it might be in Antarctica, both literally and figuratively.

Two hours later, the plane landed in Dallas, and, after a three-hour wait, Salvador and the Hardys boarded a 747 bound for Buenos Aires, Argentina.

After a twelve-hour flight, the plane landed in Argentina, and after another wait, Salvador and the Hardys boarded a 737 for Punta Arenas, Chile.

When the trio finally arrived in Punta Arenas, it was morning, a day and a half later, and Salvador took the Hardys to a place where they were able to rent the appropriate gear for the Antarctic weather. They each obtained thermal underwear, sweaters, down-filled parkas, mittens, ski masks, highly protective sunglasses, and insulated boots. Claiming the Hardys were research assistants, Salvador also made sure Frank and Joe had the necessary clearance for entering Antarctica.

Then the trio went to the tiny Punta Arenas airport, where they boarded an LC-130 transport plane, equipped with skis for Antarctic landings. Aside from Salvador and the Hardys, there were only two other passengers, both scientists.

"Exactly how far is the Antarctica shore from here?" Joe asked, as they waited for takeoff.

"About eight hundred miles," Salvador answered. "It should take a little over four hours. I can't wait for you guys to see this place. Antarctica is truly amazing. It's mostly just a chunk of ice that happens to be bigger than the entire United States."

When the plane became airborne, the engines rumbled so loudly in the cabin that conversation was almost impossible. After reading a paperback for a few hours, Joe felt the steady drone of the plane tempting him to sleep. He was not sure how long he'd dozed, but suddenly he sensed a bright light flooding through the small window beside him. Joe groggily glanced out the window. He noticed the churning gray waters of the Pacific Ocean were now sprinkled with large fragments of floating ice. Soon he spotted a stretch of white in the distance, which he realized was the shore of Antarctica.

"That's it!" Salvador called from across the aisle.

The plane began flying over the Antarctic Peninsula, a strip of land that jutted out into the ocean for several hundred miles. At one point, Joe noticed thousands of black dots peppering the ice. When the plane got closer, he could see that the black dots were actually penguins.

"All of the continent's wildlife lives near the shore," Salvador shouted to Joe. "Penguins, walruses, seals, all sorts of marine life. It seems that humans are the only ones foolish enough to go deeper inside."

"That would be us," Joe cracked.

As the plane continued over the peninsula, Joe noticed several scientific research bases, each base composed of several small buildings grouped closely together. Finally the plane approached a cluster of orange buildings that were the Argentine base of San Martín. After the LC-130 skied down to a bumpy landing, Frank, Joe, and Salvador zipped up their parkas and climbed down the plane's metal ladder.

The first thing Frank noticed was the brightness. The sun blazed in a pure blue sky, its light reflecting off the snow to create an almost unbearable whiteness. Frank put on his sunglasses. He knew that in Antarctica, the sun shone for six months without interruption, after which it was dark for six months.

Frank knelt down and ran a mitten over the slushy white surface. "That's really a mixture of snow and ice," Salvador explained. "The funny thing is, it barely snows here at all. But when it does, the snow never melts. It just packs itself down until it's ice."

Then the next thing Frank became aware of was the silence. The blanket of snowy ice that extended in every direction seemed to muffle all sound. He heard nothing but the slightest whisper of wind.

"It's really not that cold," Joe said, surprised to find he wasn't shivering.

"It's only about zero degrees, and there's very little wind right now," Salvador pointed out. "With the proper clothing, it's often quite pleasant."

Salvador led the Hardys a short distance to a hangar, where the Argentine made arrangements with a helicopter pilot he knew for transportation to Voboskov. Adding a little extra onto the fee, Salvador persuaded the pilot to go along with the cover story for getting into Voboskov.

Before long, Salvador and the Hardys were inside the helicopter, soaring beyond the peninsula into the continent. The landscape was breathtaking—a vast blanket of whiteness that shifted from flat to rolling and sometimes into strange windblown shapes known as *sastrugi*. Occasionally the chopper passed over jagged white mountains, with hints of black rock peeking through.

Frank saw no more research stations below, the bases being few and far between on the continent's gigantic interior. After an hour, though he had had plenty of rest, he felt the loud monotony of the chopper's engine lulling him to sleep.

"Misericordia!" Frank heard a voice say.

Frank was awakened by the sound of the pilot speaking nervously to himself in Spanish. With a start, Frank noticed the sky had disappeared. He could see nothing outside the helicopter, up or down, but complete whiteness. It was as if the chopper were enveloped in a gigantic wad of cotton.

"No veo nada!" the pilot said, as he pulled back on the lever to his left, lowering the chopper.

"It's a whiteout, isn't it?" Frank asked, turning to Salvador and Joe in the backseats.

"That's right," Salvador called over the chopper's buzz. "The forecast predicted clear skies, but the clouds can blow in very quickly here."

Frank could see the pilot was trying to land, an extremely dangerous proposition considering he had no idea how far away the ground was.

"Can we just hover till the whiteout fades?" Joe asked.

"We could use a lot of fuel doing that," Salvador replied. "It could prevent us from making it to Voboskov, or back to San Martín for that matter. I'm afraid we must land."

Wanting to help the pilot, Frank peered intently out the window, but all he could see was a hazy white blur. Squinting, Frank detected a small patch of blackness a short distance below the descending chopper.

Suddenly he realized the dark patch was the side of a mountain, and the chopper was angling straight for it. In several seconds the chopper's top rotor blade was going to catch that mountain, causing a certain crash.

Chapter

12

"A MOUNTAIN THIS WAY!" Frank yelled to the pilot as he pointed out his window.

"*Cómo?*" said the pilot, who didn't speak English.

There was no time to make the pilot understand. Though it was against all rules of flying protocol, Frank grabbed the lever that was between him and the pilot and pushed it away from him. Instantly the chopper banked to the left, the swirling rotor blade swinging away from the side of the mountain.

"*Vete de aqui!*" the pilot yelled at Frank.

"Tell him there's a mountain to the right!" Frank shouted at Salvador.

Salvador called a few words in Spanish to the pilot. "*Ah, sí, sí, sí,*" the pilot said as he nodded and took control of the lever.

Then the pilot shouted some instructions to Salvador, who began fishing through an emergency pack. As Salvador translated the instructions, he attached a length of rope to a red metal box. "You will take this," Salvador called to Frank, "and lower it out your door. When the box hits the ground, you will be able to judge how far away the ground is."

As the chopper hovered in place, Frank tied the rope around a metal rod. He then opened his door and tossed out the box. Moments later, he saw the red box land on the ice several hundred feet down. Keeping his eyes on the box, Frank signaled the pilot with his hand. With the pilot following Frank's instructions, the chopper soon made a safe landing on the ice.

After only twenty minutes, the clouds shifted overhead, and once again Frank saw the sun blazing against a perfectly blue sky. The chopper resumed its journey over the blindingly white terrain, and after another thirty minutes, the helicopter approached Voboskov.

Below, Frank saw three bright-blue buildings and a flagpole flying the flag of the Russian Republic. The buildings were elongated with rounded roofs, and several antennae rose from them. A satellite dish stood in front of the base, and there was a tractor parked behind it. Alone against the endless whiteness, Voboskov seemed to be the most desolate place on earth.

"Destination achieved," Salvador announced.

As the helicopter dropped vertically to the ground, Frank saw three men in red parkas emerge from one of the buildings. After a gentle landing on the ice, Frank, Joe, Salvador, and the pilot climbed out of the chopper.

"It's colder here," Joe said, feeling the shiver he had expected earlier.

"That's because we're deeper into the continent," Frank said, noticing the wind was somewhat louder than a whisper. It was more like the distant roar of an ocean crashing on the beach.

As the men in red parkas approached, one of them called out something in Russian. *"No Russke,"* Salvador called back. *"Español* or English?"

The man shook his head, indicating he did not speak either language, then beckoned for the newcomers to follow him inside. Frank, Joe, and Salvador followed the Russians to the first of the buildings while the pilot remained by the chopper.

As the Russians escorted Salvador and the Hardys down a narrow hallway lined with cardboard boxes, Joe could see there were approximately six rooms in the one-story building. Salvador and the Hardys were taken into the mess hall. Inside the well-heated room, everyone removed some of their cold-weather gear.

The mess hall was drab with no windows.

Lights hung from the curved ceiling, and the walls consisted of painted panels of plywood. The only furniture was two rectangular tables, both surrounded by metal chairs.

Almost immediately, another man stepped into the mess hall. He was a striking middle-aged man with silver hair and emerald eyes. Like the Hardys and most of the other men, he wore jeans and a sweater, but he seemed more like someone who should be wearing an expensive designer suit. Though the other men at the base had beards, this one looked as if he had shaved five minutes ago.

"Welcome to Voboskov," the man announced in flawless English. "My name is Jonathan Pless. Sergei, could we bring the guests some tea, please?"

So this was Jonathan Pless, Joe thought. The research-and-development chief of IDEA, a man whom Interpol suspected of espionage and murder, all in the name of profit. Joe figured Pless would not be at the base unless there was something important going on. He could tell the man was wary of the unexpected guests. He and Frank had combed their hair differently, and Frank had covered the wound between his eyes with some makeup purchased in an airport gift shop.

"Hello," Salvador said, moving to shake Pless's hand. "Sorry for just dropping in like this. We were headed for the Belgano III base, but we experienced some minor helicopter problems. We figured we'd stop here to let the pilot do the repair work. He's out there now. He shouldn't be long."

"And who exactly are you?" Pless inquired.

"I'm Antonio Salvador, a geophysicist from the University of New Mexico," Salvador explained. "This is Jim and Jerry Blanders. They are brothers and also graduate students here to assist me. It's their first time in Antarctica."

Pless's suspicion seemed to ease into politeness. "Well, make yourselves comfortable," he said, taking a seat at the table.

Joe noticed that one of the Russians had gone into the kitchen while the other two lingered in the mess hall. The Russians all seemed like rugged types, and Joe had to wonder if they were scientists or thugs hired to guard Weinhardt.

"You don't seem to be a Russian," Frank said as he, Joe, and Salvador also took seats at the table.

"That's because I'm not," Pless replied. "I'm Swiss, actually. I head up the R-and-D department for a company known as International Development Engineering Associates."

"I see," Frank said, playing the role of an interested grad student. "If I may ask, what are you doing down here? After all, it's a long way from Switzerland."

Pless pulled a large silver coin from his pocket and began twirling it between his fingers as he spoke. "The economy in Russia has been so poor lately that they cannot afford to maintain all their Antarctic bases," Pless explained. "So my company has stepped in as part of our 'good neighbor' policy. We have donated a sum of money to maintain this station, and I am here, well, just for a brief visit."

"I didn't think private companies were allowed to do business in Antarctica," Frank mentioned.

"They're not," Pless said, switching the coin to his other hand. "My company is *contributing* money to the station, not investing it. Like many large corporations, we also contribute to third-world countries, charities, scholarships, and other worthy causes. It's a nice thing to do and it's also a healthy tax write-off."

"This base is smaller than some of the others I've seen," Frank remarked.

"Yes, it's only three buildings," Pless pointed out. "This building contains the mess hall, rec rooms, and storage areas. The next building over contains the science laboratories. And the farthest building contains the living quarters."

"How many people work here?" Frank asked.

"Eight at the moment," Pless answered. "Six scientists, one engineer, and a cook. All Russian."

The group continued chatting pleasantly another few minutes. All signs indicated Pless was buying the cover story, which meant it was time for Joe to have a look around for Kenneth

Weinhardt. Just as Joe stood, a piercing whistle sounded.

"Ah, tea time," Pless said, pocketing his silver coin. "Even here, we must not forget civilization."

"I have a very important question about this base," Joe said. "Which way is the men's room?"

"There's one at the end of the hallway," Pless replied with a smile. "You can't miss it."

Oh, yes I can, Joe thought as he stepped out of the room. After passing two doors, he saw a corridor, which he could see led to the next building. Based on Pless's words, Joe assumed the next building over contained the labs.

When Joe stole a glance back at the mess hall, he was dismayed to see one of the Russians watching him. The Russian pointed a finger at the end of the hall, and Joe nodded. As he walked toward the rest room, Joe realized he might not be free to explore the base after all.

He opened a door and stepped inside a rest room. After shutting the door, he pulled a string, turning on a light. Joe noticed there was a trapdoor on the floor and remembered seeing one in the mess hall as well.

Lifting the trapdoor, he saw a space two feet deep and filled with a tangle of rubber-wrapped electrical cables. Joe realized it was a sub-floor that probably ran throughout the entire base. Chances were, every single room had a trapdoor for easy access to the cables.

Joe slipped onto the sub-floor and pulled the trapdoor back into place. Though the sub-floor was pitch-dark, tiny cracks of light spilled through here and there, and Joe realized it was coming from the rooms with lights on at the moment.

Crawling on his belly, maneuvering past the spaghetti of cables, Joe made his way toward the lab building, figuring that would be the best place to start his search for Weinhardt. The sub-floor was cold and cramped, but soon Joe reached the lab building, where he could see the lights were on in only a single room.

Joe crawled directly underneath the lit room and found another trapdoor. Above he heard voices. Awkwardly propping himself on one elbow, Joe pushed the trapdoor up—very slowly, just an inch. He saw two pairs of sneakers on the floor. Ever so slowly and quietly, Joe eased the trapdoor a few inches higher. In the center of the room stood a long counter, upon which sat lab apparatus and several high-tech machines.

A young man with light blond hair was standing at the counter, and another man was sitting at a computer. The second man's back was to Joe, but he could see the man wore a flannel shirt, corduroys, and had wild grayish hair. Could it be Weinhardt? The hair color was right, Joe saw, remembering the photo of the physicist Irene had given him and Frank.

Suddenly the man at the computer turned to the blond guy.

Joe saw the man's face. Even though the man had a beard, Joe recognized the round, friendly Santa Claus face of Kenneth Weinhardt. The man even wore the same wire-rimmed glasses Weinhardt wore in the photograph.

Joe felt his heart speed up as he realized the mission was accomplished. He thought of Irene, wishing for a moment that she could have come along on the trip. She would have been so happy to find her father.

It was certain—Jonathan Pless was the villain in this case. Joe, Frank, and Salvador needed to make a graceful exit as soon as possible so they could notify the proper authorities.

But then the blond man noticed the trapdoor was slightly lifted.

Joe froze, knowing if he lowered the trapdoor, he would give himself away. He hoped the man would think someone had lifted the door for electrical maintenance and not replaced it properly.

Joe held his breath as the blond man walked over to the trapdoor. The blond man knelt down—then suddenly flipped the door upward, exposing Joe.

"Who are you?" the blond man barked. Though the man spoke English, Joe detected a Russian accent.

"What is it, Gregor?" Weinhardt said, turning to the commotion on the floor.

"It seems we have an intruder," Gregor told Weinhardt. "Call for help."

"No, wait," Joe said, standing up. "I can explain. My companions and I had helicopter trouble, and we stopped at the base for repairs. I was just having a look around. When I saw this underground tunnel I, uh . . ."

There was an intercom system on the wall, and Joe saw Weinhardt press a button on it.

"Attention," Weinhardt spoke into the mike. "We have an intruder—"

"No, don't!" Joe whispered to Weinhardt as he climbed out of the sub-floor. "I'm here to help! If you do that, it'll ruin everything!"

The blond man grabbed Joe by the shoulders.

"We have an intruder in Lab 2," Weinhardt continued into the mike, keeping his eyes on Joe. "I repeat. There is an intruder in Lab 2. Please send assistance at once!"

"Professor Weinhardt, listen to me," Joe urged as Weinhardt released the button. "I know what's happened to you, and I've come to help you get out of here. I'm a friend of Irene."

"My daughter?" Weinhardt asked, confused.

"Yes," Joe said. "Now you have to say you were mistaken. Say you saw this blond guy come in and you thought he was the intruder. Meanwhile I'll sneak out the way I came. Please, Professor. If you don't do this, and I'm caught, no one will ever know you're here!"

"But you see," Weinhardt stated, "I don't want anyone to know I'm here." Behind the man's glasses, Joe saw something in Weinhardt's eyes that did not seem so friendly.

Then three Russians barged into the room, each clutching an automatic pistol.

Chapter

13

IMMEDIATELY JOE raised his hands. The next moment Pless hurried into the lab, followed by Frank and Salvador. "What's going on?" Pless asked, glancing at Joe.

"This boy says he has come to help rescue me," Weinhardt answered. "He knows my daughter, and he seems to know exactly who I am."

Pless looked at Joe, then Frank. Suddenly the polished Swiss executive lost his composure. "I've been a fool!" Pless cried, slapping a hand on the counter. "You boys aren't Jim and Jerry Blanders. You're Frank and Joe Hardy, the ones who have been working with Irene Weinhardt. My men gave me descriptions of you. I just didn't expect you to show up at my doorstep so quickly!"

"Everyone makes mistakes," Frank offered.

"And who are you?" Pless demanded of Salvador.

Salvador looked at Frank for guidance. "There's a little more to this than we told you," Frank said to Salvador. "I'm sorry now that we got you involved. You'd better tell this man who you are."

"I am exactly who I said I was," Salvador informed Pless. "I met these boys two days ago and offered to help them get to Antarctica."

Pless let out a deep sigh, then briefly massaged the bridge of his nose. "So now you know," Pless told the Hardys, turning calmer. "Professor Weinhardt is working here at Voboskov. But what you apparently don't know is this: he is here of his own volition!"

"I'm not sure I believe that," Frank challenged.

Pless said something in Russian. The three Russians put their pistols away, then quickly frisked Frank, Joe, and Salvador. They found no weapons and conveyed this to Pless in their native language.

"Ken, I think you had better tell these three the truth," Pless told Weinhardt. "I know you are extremely busy, but this is important."

During the entire interrogation, Weinhardt had been drumming his fingers on the counter. The physicist looked haggard and unhappy, and Frank wondered if Weinhardt was drumming his fingers because he was a frightened prisoner being forced to say something or because he was impatient to return to work.

"All right," Weinhardt said. "Very briefly, the story is this. While working at Los Alamos, I discovered a compound that would superconduct at temperatures substantially higher than absolute zero—two hundred twenty degrees Kelvin, to be precise. But I wasn't satisfied. I felt there must be a way to adjust the compound so it would work at a much higher temperature."

"Then what happened," Pless prompted.

"Two things," Weinhardt explained. "I was having trouble solving the problem, and also the government began keeping my findings top-secret because they were planning to use them on weapons technology. Well, this was very distasteful to me, so I left Los Alamos and took a teaching job at Bayport University. But then one day I got a call from Mr. Pless. We had spoken before, but this time he had rather important news."

"And what was that?" Pless asked.

"Mr. Pless explained how he was funding research here at the Voboskov base," Weinhardt continued. "He also explained how a geologist here, quite by accident, discovered that the same compound I was working with was superconducting down here at temperatures much higher than what I had achieved."

If Weinhardt is being forced to lie, Frank thought, he's doing an excellent job of it.

"This was very interesting to me," Weinhardt

continued, "because I had speculated myself that perhaps the unique magnetic conditions of Antarctica could alter the effects of superconductors and perhaps teach us a few things about the nature of superconductivity. Anyway, I realized if I could come down here and experiment in this environment, I might find a way to make my compound superconduct at higher temperatures in other environments as well."

"This is all fascinating," Joe spoke up. "But what about the fact that you're supposedly dead?"

"I'm afraid the plot thickens a bit," Weinhardt said, adjusting his glasses. "I was sure the government was watching me after I left Los Alamos. They were wary of me doing my superconductivity work with another country or organization, and I knew they would especially not like me coming to a Russian base in Antarctica—even though my reasons for doing so would be purely scientific."

"So you faked your own death?" Frank asked.

"Yes," Weinhardt confirmed. "Mr. Pless arranged everything, but it was actually my idea. You see, I knew this would be the only way I could work in Antarctica in peace."

"What about your family?" Joe asked. "Didn't you think they might be upset about your death?"

"I realize it was cruel of me to fool them this way," Weinhardt said, removing his glasses to rub his eyes. "But I simply could not let anyone know where I was. If I did, the U.S. government would most likely find out about it."

"You were that determined to make this breakthrough?" Frank wanted to know.

"I ask you," Weinhardt said, "how often does a man get the chance to change the world? To come up with some scientific discovery that will make life on earth easier, better, more intelligent? To do such a thing is every scientist's dream. Unfortunately, living in complete secrecy down here is the only way I can achieve this dream. So this is what I must do. And when I am done here I will return to my family."

"I see," Frank said. It made sense. Irene had said Weinhardt often seemed more interested in his work than his own family. She didn't believe Weinhardt would go so far as to fake his own death for the sake of his research, but then what daughter would want to admit that about her father? Frank decided Professor Weinhardt was probably telling the truth.

Then Frank's eyes fell on a machine sitting on the counter—a shiny cylinder protruding from a black frame. Frank realized it was a device similar to the one that had attracted his watch at Los Alamos. "It's a super-magnet," Weinhardt said, noticing Frank staring at the device.

"It sure is," Frank commented.

Weinhardt chuckled, though Frank wasn't quite sure why. "Tell me," Weinhardt said, suddenly seeming more friendly and relaxed, "how is my family?"

"They're fine," Joe said, a touch of reprimand in his voice. "But they miss you."

"Since you're friends with Irene," Weinhardt said, a smile creeping across his lips, "I will tell you one very amusing thing about her, then I must get back to work. One day when Irene was around, oh, twelve, she was doing a chemistry experiment in the kitchen, and she caused this tremendous explosion. Well, from then on, whenever I heard a loud bang in the house, I would come running like mad into the kitchen. It became something of a family joke."

Weinhardt chuckled at the memory and seemed disappointed the Hardys weren't sharing the humor. "Do you understand," Weinhardt said, leaning closer to Frank. "Whenever I heard a loud bang in the house, I would come running!" Weinhardt chuckled again.

"I understand," Frank said. At least he seems to have some feelings for his daughter, he thought.

"Shall we go?" Pless said as Weinhardt began typing at his keyboard. Frank, Joe, Salvador, the three Russians, and Pless filed out of the laboratory, Pless closing the door behind them.

"What are you going to do with us now?" Salvador asked, glancing nervously at the Russians.

"I am going to challenge one of you to a game of Ping-Pong," Pless announced. "Follow me."

The group walked in silence back toward the first building. Pless still wasn't to be trusted, Frank thought. Weinhardt might be here by choice, but even so, Pless had tried to kill him, Joe, and Irene, to keep them from knowing about it.

When the group reached the first building, the Russians peeled off, and Pless ushered Salvador and the Hardys into a recreation room. It contained a worn couch, a shelf of books, a TV and VCR, a small pool table, and a Ping-Pong table. Frank also noticed posters of Russian movies on the wall.

"Ping-Pong is a favorite pastime around here," Pless said, closing the door. "It will also give us a chance for a serious chat. Who wants to take me on? I'll warn you, I'm fairly good."

"I'll play," Frank said, thinking it could buy some time while he tried to figure out what Pless was up to.

Pless and Frank picked up paddles and took their places at opposite sides of the table. Joe stood by the pool table while Salvador stood near the door. For a few moments, Frank and Pless volleyed the ball between them, each hit causing a hollow little click. Joe heard another sound and realized it was the wind, which had picked up considerably outside.

"First, tell me," Pless said, sending a nice spin ball to Frank, "are you convinced Kenneth Weinhardt is here completely on his own volition?"

"I guess so," Frank said, returning the ball.

"Good," Pless said. "Obviously the professor and myself wish for his presence here to remain a secret. I have taken extreme and, yes, illegal, measures to keep it so. I had the phone tapped at the Weinhardt home. When I discovered Irene and the two of you were looking for Professor Weinhardt, I had men try to scare you away. However, I assure you, it was never their intention to kill anyone."

"You could have fooled me," Joe remarked.

"I know," Pless admitted. "I am sorry for the fright I have given you, but the professor's work here is very important. You understand that, don't you?"

"I suppose so," Frank said, sending the ball to Pless's outside right corner.

"Now," Pless said, easily returning the shot, "I have given you the truth, and you must do the same for me. I must know if you boys have told anyone, aside from Irene, that you suspected Professor Weinhardt was in Antarctica."

"Aside from Irene," Frank replied, "we haven't told anyone. Honest."

Pless glanced at Joe. "He's telling the truth," Joe confirmed.

With unexpected force, Pless slammed a shot that Frank could not return.

"Excellent," Pless said. "And I know you two will keep this little secret. Forever."

"They certainly will" came a strange voice.

Joe looked over and discovered it was Salvador who had spoken. But Joe realized that instead of an Argentine accent, Salvador had just spoken with a Russian accent. "What gives?" Joe said slowly.

"As they say in the States"—Salvador spoke again in the Russian accent—"you have taken the bait. Hook, line, and sinker."

Frank dropped his paddle on the table. "They've trapped us, Joe," he said, forcing himself to remain calm. "Salvador brought us here at the request of Jonathan Pless."

"But . . ." Joe said, thoroughly confused.

"Let's hear it, Frank," Pless said, twirling his paddle. "I want to see how good a detective you are."

"Okay, uh . . . let me see," Frank said, willing to entertain the man if it bought more time. "After Pless, or Cosmo, discovered it was me, not Orion, talking to him on the computer, he knew I had enough information to figure out Weinhardt was in Antarctica. Pless needed to know if we reported this to anyone besides Irene. So he changed his strategy. Instead of having his men try to kill us, he got Salvador, or whatever his real name is, to bring us down here for questioning."

"The whole thing was a setup!" Joe said, pounding a fist on the pool table. "They *wanted* me to sneak off and find Weinhardt. They coached Weinhardt on what to say, and I'm sure they threatened to kill off his whole family if he didn't comply."

"Weinhardt *is* being held against his will," Frank said. "But Pless needed us to believe otherwise so we would trust him enough to tell him the truth. And we just did. He had to find out who else suspected Weinhardt was still alive."

"I have to admit," Pless said, setting his paddle down, "you boys show signs of talent. Nevertheless, you are amateurs playing against professionals. And now that the professionals have won the game, it is time for the losers to die."

Joe realized he and Frank would be executed in a matter of minutes, but neither Salvador nor Pless seemed to be armed at the moment. If he and Frank could take them temporarily out of commission, that might buy a little extra time to come up with an escape plan.

Pool cues hung on a rack right behind Joe. In one swift movement, he grabbed a cue and swung the thick end of it straight for Salvador's Adam's apple. But Salvador grabbed the cue and yanked Joe closer with it before Joe could let go.

Then Salvador's fist shot out. Just in time, Joe turned his head, trading a broken nose for a stinging cheek. Ignoring the pain, he ploughed a shoulder into Salvador's stomach, driving the Russian up against the wall.

Pless had already made a move for the intercom box on the wall, but Frank sent a quick judo kick into the box, destroying it. Pless backed away from Frank, obviously not a man fond of physical violence.

Frank turned to see Salvador jerk his knee upward into Joe's chin. As Joe's head flinched backward, Salvador slugged Joe in the stomach, sending him reeling into the pool table.

Frank was in motion, lifting off the ground to send one of his big boots straight for Salvador's face. But Salvador caught Frank's leg as easily as he had the pool cue, then swung Frank in a half circle. When he let go, Frank went flying across the room until he slammed into the plywood wall.

Frank sat up, his back throbbing, and noticed Joe sitting by the pool table, dazed and spitting out blood. Pless hovered in a corner of the room, waiting to see if the roughhousing was over. Salvador stood proudly over the scene, barely winded.

The Hardys were top-notch fighters, but Frank realized Salvador was in a different class. Muscle alone wasn't going to get them out of their dire situation.

The wind was howling now, blowing so hard it banged loudly against the walls of the building.

"Salvador," Joe said, not bothering to conceal his contempt. "Besides being a filthy, despicable liar, who are you?"

"My name is Andrei Sorsky," the man said flatly. "I am a former agent of the KGB, as are most of the other men here at the base. Same for the two men who followed you from Bayport to New Mexico. Same for the helicopter pilot. We all work for Pless now."

"Are you guys also available for parties?" Joe said, wiping blood from his lip.

"Any party that pays," Sorsky returned.

Now that Sorsky was speaking with his natural voice and accent, he sounded familiar to Frank. "You're Orion, aren't you?" Frank asked Sorsky. "The one who followed me and Irene to the mission."

"That is correct," the man named Sorsky said. "I am also the one who is going to kill you— right now. Any more questions?"

Chapter

14

SORSKY OPENED THE DOOR and shouted a few words in Russian. A moment later, four of the ex-KGB men entered the room, one of them being the helicopter pilot. They all carried automatic pistols.

Joe saw the pilot hand his weapon to Sorsky and tried desperately to think of a way out of the situation, which was becoming increasingly grim. Sorsky alone was tough enough, but now the Hardys faced four more of the well-trained KGB men, not to mention the guns. Joe tried his best not to panic.

"Before you shoot, Andrei, I will leave," Pless said, heading for the door.

"This will be painless," Sorsky said, calmly pointing his pistol at Frank.

"Irene Weinhardt knows we're here," Frank called to Pless. "If we don't return to the States soon, people will come looking for us."

Pless stopped, halfway to the door. "My men in New Mexico are monitoring her every move," he informed Frank. "So far, I don't believe she has told anyone where you are. In fact, you probably advised her not to. My men will execute Miss Weinhardt the first chance they get. She seems to be sticking very close to her classmates, but my men are both patient and skillful. Lucky for me, the KGB went out of business." Pless resumed walking to the door.

Pless had to pass right by Joe to get out the door. Another step and—Joe quickly flung his right arm around Pless's neck, catching the man in a choke-hold. "You imbecile," Pless said, struggling to pull Joe's arm away. "What are you doing?"

Two of the Russians pointed their guns at Joe while Sorsky kept his gun on Frank. "Let him go," Sorsky ordered Joe. "Nothing will save you."

"Maybe not," Joe said, keeping Pless's body between himself and the guns. "Here's the deal though. I can break Mr. Pless's neck in exactly two seconds with a twist in just the right spot. Matter of fact, it's an old KGB trick. I'm sure a few of you are quite familiar with it."

For a moment there was no sound except that

of the wind banging against the walls of the building.

"Doubtful," Sorsky said.

"I assure you, I can," Joe said, gripping Pless's neck tighter. "Now, I want Mr. Pilot over there to give my brother the keys to the chopper. Tell him, Sorsky. In Russian or Spanish, take your choice."

Sorsky kept the pistol on Frank, saying nothing.

Joe gave a little twist to Pless's neck.

"Owww," Pless groaned. "Tell him, Andrei."

Sorsky muttered something in Russian to the helicopter pilot. The pilot grudgingly pulled a set of keys from his pocket and tossed them at Frank.

"Good," Joe said. "Frank, get all of our gear from the mess hall, then start the chopper up. When I hear the engine, I'll come join you."

"Weinhardt?" Frank asked.

"We don't have time," Joe said. "But they won't dare kill him if we're out free. You don't want a murder that *can* be proven, do you, Mr. Pless?"

As Frank darted from the room, Joe saw one of the Russians start to slip away. "Stay where you are!" Joe called to the man. The Russian looked at Sorsky, and Sorsky nodded. The man stayed.

As Joe kept his arm around Pless, all the Russians glared at Joe with hateful eyes. If looks could kill, Joe thought, I would be dead, but they can't and I'm not. Over the wind's wild banging, Joe heard an exterior door open and close. Moments later—though it seemed like hours to Joe—he heard the chopper roar to life outside.

"Everybody stay right here," Joe instructed, "or else Pless dies. Then nobody gets paid." Keeping his arm firmly around Pless's neck, Joe backed out of the room, the Russians stepping out of Joe's way.

Joe escorted Pless down the hallway, glad to see no one was following. "This is not going to work," Pless growled at Joe. "I guarantee you won't get away."

When Joe came to the exterior door, he opened it with his left hand. A ferocious blast of wind poured inside. Through a haze of blowing snow, Joe could see the helicopter's rotors were already spinning, ready for takeoff. "Mr. Pless," Joe said, shoving the man roughly to the floor, "never mess with amateurs!"

Gritting his teeth against the biting cold, Joe made a dash for the chopper. As he climbed inside, Frank opened the throttle and the chopper ascended.

Chilled to the bone, Joe quickly pulled on his parka and mask, noticing Frank was already wearing his. Before the chopper was fifty feet off the ground, Joe saw six Russians emerge from the base, wearing parkas and carrying guns.

"They've got pistols," Joe yelled over the din of the turbine engine and roaring wind.

"Pistols should be no problem," Frank called, now angling the chopper forward as it ascended. "I don't know how far we'll get in this wind, but I'll try to get us far enough."

"I'd appreciate that," Joe said, pulling on his mittens. Then he saw Sorsky emerge from the base, aiming an assault rifle at the chopper, which was now about a hundred feet high and flying away from the base. "Move it, Frank!" Joe shouted. "Sorsky's got an AK-47!"

Knowing the Russian-made long-distance weapon could probably snag them, Frank swung the chopper onto its side as he continued lifting. Then he swung the other way, keeping the target moving.

Though Joe couldn't hear Sorsky's gun, he knew it was releasing an incredibly rapid barrage of bullets into the air. Suddenly the helicopter's engine was screaming at a high pitch.

"Get us out of range!" Joe shouted as he watched the Russians grow smaller in the distance.

"We're almost out now!" Frank yelled. "But Sorsky hit the engine. That's bad."

"We're still flying," Joe called back. "Just get us as far as you can."

"Take a look at the damage," Frank instructed.

When Joe craned his head for a look through the back window, he saw black smoke streaming from the chopper's rear. "There's smoke coming from the engine!" Joe reported.

Immediately Frank closed down the throttle, causing the chopper to cut altitude. "Sorry," Frank said, "but we have to bail."

"Can't we go just a bit farther?" Joe asked.

"No," Frank said, unstrapping his seat belt. "If the engine is smoking, this thing is going to be a fire ball any second. I've brought us down a bit. Open your door and jump!"

Joe opened his door and glanced down. Through the swirling snow, it was impossible to judge how far away the ground was, but it really didn't matter. Joe had no choice but to jump. Without further delay, he lunged into the wind.

Frank remembered there was an emergency pack in the chopper, which he found under a rear seat. He opened his door and tossed out the pack. Then he pulled on his mittens and jumped. He felt his stomach doing crazy back flips as he plunged through the roaring air. After several seconds that seemed like several hours, he pounded onto the icy surface.

Frank lay on the ground a moment, letting the shock subside. Then he noticed Joe lying on the ground several yards away. "Are you okay?" Frank called over the wind.

"Swell," Joe said, sitting up. "These parkas make pretty good padding. I'll have to remember that next time I jump from a flaming helicopter."

Something exploded in the distance, and Frank

realized the helicopter had blown. When the chopper was silent, Frank understood how amazingly loud the wind was. It sounded as if it were blaring from a gargantuan sound system with treble and bass both turned up to max.

Squinting to see through the heavy gauze of snow, Frank made out the bright-blue shapes of the Voboskov base, only about a hundred yards away. He saw no sign of the Russians. "They don't seem to be coming after us," Frank called.

"I wonder why not," Joe shouted back.

"No need," Frank replied. "With the wind chill, it's probably sixty below right now. The cold will kill us just fine and they know it."

"There's a tractor at the base, maybe we can—"

"Forget it," Frank interrupted. "There's not another station for at least a hundred miles. We would never make it. Our only chance is to climb inside the ice and try to wait out the storm."

Frank found the emergency pack lying nearby, which he opened, pulling out an ice ax and a small shovel. He had hoped to find food, matches, and an emergency stove, but they were missing.

Using the ax, Frank chopped at a section of ice, loosening it up, then Joe worked at the same section with the shovel, carving out an opening. The Hardys continued this process for nearly a half hour until they had formed a trench just large enough for both of them to squeeze into.

By the time they nestled into the trench, both Hardys were shivering violently with cold. It was slightly warmer inside the trench but not by much. The wind showed no signs of slowing, and each time a wave of it blew by, they felt the chill rip through all their layers of clothing like a sharp knife.

"I don't think I've ever been this cold," Joe said through chattering teeth.

"Let's talk about something," Frank suggested. "Maybe we can keep our minds from realizing how miserable our bodies are."

"Okay," Joe said. "Uh, let's see . . . well, tell me this. Was Sorsky in New Mexico the whole time we were there?"

"Probably," Frank replied. "He just kept a low profile so we didn't see him—until he wanted us to. After we escaped from his hotel room, he probably sent the other two goons to pick up our trail. Then he contacted Pless, and Pless figured out it was me on the other end of that computer conversation. Then Pless told Sorsky to bring us to Antarctica."

"And Sorsky knew we would go to Antarctica if there was a practical way to do it," Joe figured. "So he created Antonio Salvador."

"Well, Sorsky knew we had never seen his face," Frank said, "so he didn't need a disguise."

"So the goons trail us to that cafe and they contact Sorsky," Joe figured. "Then Sorsky shows up, except now he's the friendly Antonio Salvador."

"And while Salvador is talking to us in the club," Frank said, "the two goons put the nitro-filled piñata in the van. That gives Salvador a chance to prove to us he's not a bad guy."

"I hate to say it," Joe said, "but those KGB guys are pretty impressive."

"Hey, that reminds me," Frank said. "Do you really know how to break someone's neck in two seconds?"

"No," Joe said. "But if they can lie to us, I can . . . lie to . . ."

"What's the matter?" Frank asked.

"I'm having trouble getting my . . . my mouth to work," Joe answered.

Frank didn't like what he was hearing. Difficulty in speaking was one of the signs of hypothermia. He glanced at the furiously blowing snow, wondering when the wind was going to stop.

"Professor Wein . . ." Joe said. "Professor Wein . . ."

"What?" Frank asked.

"I wonder what he . . ." Joe tried to say. "What he likes . . . for dinner."

Frank realized Joe's thoughts were becoming jumbled, another sign of hypothermia. As he wrapped his arms around Joe to give his brother more warmth, Frank shut his eyes, struggling to come up with a solution. But there simply were no other options. He and Joe might have been a match for Pless and his men, but nobody was a match against the monstrous fury of an Antarctic wind.

"I wonder . . ." Joe attempted to say.

"Don't talk," Frank said. He could see that Joe's teeth were chattering uncontrollably beneath his ski mask. Joe was getting worse by the second.

The wind shrieked louder, now sounding like a wounded animal caught in a trap, desperately crying for help.

There was no escaping the truth. Frank realized that very soon he and his brother were going to freeze to death.

Chapter

15

STILL HUDDLED in the icy trench, Frank heard a sharp burst of sound.

"What . . . was that?" Joe asked.

"I don't know!" Frank answered. "It came from the direction of the base."

A moment later, Frank heard another similar sound, which he realized was an explosion. Suddenly a phrase jumped into Frank's mind: "Whenever I heard a loud bang I would come running."

Then Frank heard another explosion.

"Wait, I think that was a signal from Weinhardt!" Frank cried out. "Come on!" Frank hoisted himself out of the hollow, then helped Joe out. They charged against the wind, running toward the blue buildings of the base.

"Weinhardt said something to me, but I didn't get it till now," Frank called as he ran. "Remember when he was telling me about Irene? He said she once caused an explosion in the kitchen. After that, he said, whenever he heard a loud bang in the house, he would come running. Then he repeated the phrase. I think he meant for us to come running as soon as we heard a loud bang!"

As the Hardys approached the base, Frank saw someone standing and waving in the doorway of the first building. Through blowing snow he recognized the wild hair and beard of Kenneth Weinhardt.

"Thank goodness you understood my signal," Weinhardt said as Frank and Joe hurried into the building. The physicist led the Hardys into the mess hall, where he made them take off their coats and masks.

"What did you do?" Frank asked.

"I caused some explosions in the lab," Weinhardt said, handing Frank and Joe each a candy bar. "Just a little bit of fire, a lot of smoke, and a few loud booms. They're all in there now, putting out the flames. I'm sorry it took so long, but Pless had several men watching me after you left the lab."

"Is there a radio or phone nearby?" Frank asked, feeling his body warmth return in the well-heated room.

"There's a communications room in the lab

building, but it's kept locked," Weinhardt answered.

"I can probably break in," Frank said. "Then I can send an SOS. How are you doing, Joe?"

"Much better," Joe said, chewing his candy bar.

"The problem is," Weinhardt said, "it will take hours for help to arrive. But I have a plan that will help us take control of the base. Are you two warm enough to proceed?"

Frank and Joe both nodded. Weinhardt led the Hardys down the hallway and through the corridor leading to the lab building. "When I saw you boys, I knew you could assist me if only I could come up with a plan," Weinhardt explained. "It all came to me when I saw Frank looking at the super-magnet. You see, we can use it to draw the guns and the men, all of whom wear watches. I didn't use the magnet earlier because not all the men were present, and you would not have known to help me get the guns when they fell."

They had now reached the lab building, which was filled with black smoke and a strong burning smell. "There's the com room," Weinhardt whispered to Frank, pointing to a door. "Joe, come with me. Oh, yes, remove your watch, please."

Frank headed for the communications room to send out an SOS, while Joe followed Weinhardt to Lab 2. Joe waited outside the door as Weinhardt entered the room.

"What happened?" Joe heard Pless ask Weinhardt.

"I don't know," Weinhardt said, coughing and acting the scatterbrained professor. "Perhaps one of my magnesium compounds spontaneously combusted."

Joe stole a look inside the room. Through a dense fog of black smoke, he counted eleven men, including Weinhardt, Pless, and Sorsky. Some of them were still holding fire extinguishers, looking around for any lingering trace of flame.

"Now!" Weinhardt shouted as he flipped a switch.

At once, the lab was filled with shouts as everyone present, except for Joe and Weinhardt, was jerked by their wristwatch toward the powerful super-magnet. Entering the room, Joe saw four pistols fly onto the mirrorlike cylinder.

"Now!" Weinhardt called, reversing the switch.

Instantly everyone was released from the magnet. The four pistols clanged to the floor, and before anyone else could react, Joe kicked them toward Weinhardt. The professor grabbed them, stuffed three of them into his jacket pockets, and held the fourth pointed toward the men.

"Everyone lie on the ground!" Joe commanded. "Hands behind your heads!"

"If anyone resists, I won't hesitate to kill!" Weinhardt added. Then he repeated the order in Russian, and everyone obeyed.

Once all the men were down, Joe took a head count. His heart sank when he realized two were missing—Sorsky and Pless. With all the smoke and confusion, they had slipped out without Joe spotting them.

Weinhardt found some rope, and Joe tied the men securely while the professor kept a pistol on them.

"I'll stay here and keep an eye on them," Joe said when the task was finished. "You go guard the com room for Frank. We've got to get off that message!"

The com room contained a cellular telephone, a computer, and a shortwave radio set. The cellular phone wasn't functioning because of the storm, and Frank didn't have anyone standing by for an E-mail message. The radio was the only hope, and even that would be difficult because of the weather.

Sitting at a desk, wearing a headset, Frank was slowly turning a dial on the radio, searching for an active frequency. But so far he'd gotten only static.

Suddenly Frank saw Weinhardt in the doorway, holding a gun. "We've got all the men contained except for Sorsky and Pless," the physicist reported. "They escaped. Joe told me to guard you."

"Stay right by the door," Frank said. "If you see anyone approach, do what you have to."

"Right," Weinhardt said, returning to the hallway.

Then, through the static, Frank heard the faintest trace of a voice. "Come in, please!" Frank pleaded into his headset, easing the dial to the right. "This is a Mayday! I repeat, this is a Mayday!"

"Hello," a dim voice crackled back. "This is the U.S. Coast Guard at McMurdo. Can you hear me?"

"Just barely," Frank said. "Can you hear me?"

"Barely," the voice answered. "Where are you?"

Frank was about to answer when a trapdoor in the room flew open—and Andrei Sorsky shot out of it, clutching an automatic pistol.

Frank dove behind the desk, pulling the radio with him, as a series of bullets furiously exploded, ringing and ripping through the metal of the desk. Frank heard a second gun firing on top of the first, the noise in the room now deafening.

Then the room fell silent.

Frank held his breath and listened, hearing nothing but the blank static in his headset and the howling wind outside. He stole a peek around the side of the desk.

Sorsky, his face blackened from smoke, was backed against the wall and pointing his gun at the desk. Weinhardt, glasses hanging off his frightened face, was pointing his gun at Sorsky. There was also a popping and sizzling sound in the room and then the overhead light started flickering.

"If you fire one more shot," Weinhardt told Sorsky, breathing hard, "I will kill you."

A smile formed on Sorsky's lips. "I do not think so," Sorsky said. "Professor, I believe you lack what it takes to kill a man."

As the wind howled and the lights flickered, the two men glared at each other—the peace-loving scientist and the professional killer. To Weinhardt's credit, Frank feared Sorsky was right about the physicist. But Frank also noticed a look of determination in Weinhardt's eyes that reminded him of Irene.

"I think I will kill you first, Professor," Sorsky said, swinging his gun to Weinhardt. "And then I will kill the Hardy boy."

Frank realized he had to give Weinhardt an advantage somehow, but his mind was as blank as the static in his ears. Suddenly it came to him. "Hello, Coast Guard," he suddenly spoke, pulling off his headset. "I don't have much—"

It worked. Believing Frank was really communicating with someone, Sorsky moved for the desk, and at the same time, a short series of gun-shots exploded through the room.

"Ahhhh!" Sorsky yelled as he fell against the wall, dropping his gun and gripping his right shoulder.

"Nice shot, Professor," Frank said, noticing Weinhardt had hit Sorsky's gun arm in several places. It was exactly what an FBI marksman would have done.

Weinhardt said nothing, only nodding.

By the flickering light, Frank saw Sorsky wince with pain, blood running through his fingers. Then the ex-KGB man turned to Frank, a strange look on his face, and said, "I hope there's no hard feelings. Please understand, I was only doing my job."

"Andrei," Frank said evenly, "there's plenty of hard feelings.

While Weinhardt kept his gun on Sorsky, Frank knelt by the radio, put on the headset, and searched for the frequency he had found earlier. "Hello," Frank said, adjusting the dial. "McMurdo, are you there? McMurdo, do you read me?"

"McMurdo," a voice responded. "Where are you?"

After Frank conveyed the vital information to McMurdo, he and Weinhardt escorted Sorsky to the lab, where Joe was still standing guard over his eight prisoners. Weinhardt kept watch while Frank and Joe went off to search for Pless.

It didn't take long. When Joe and Frank got to the first building, they noticed a door was open, the furious wind whipping through the hallway. They saw a bundled figure riding through the wildly swirling snow on a snowmobile. If anything, the storm was more intense than before.

"Think we should go after him?" Joe asked,

figuring there must be other snowmobiles stored somewhere.

Frank watched Pless disappear into the unforgiving whiteness, shook his head, and said, "Nah. The cold will get him first."

When they returned to the lab, the smoke had died down and Weinhardt had put dressings on Sorsky's bullet wounds. Frank, Joe, and Weinhardt took seats in the room and watched the prisoners at gunpoint. There was nothing left to do but wait for help.

"You know," Weinhardt said, glancing at the automatic pistol in his hand, "I don't like weapons very much."

"So we've been told," Joe said.

"Now, tell us, Professor," Frank said, keeping a careful eye on the prisoners, "how did you really get mixed up with Pless?"

"He had spies at Los Alamos," Weinhardt explained. "Among other things, the spies were keeping abreast of my work with superconductivity. When Pless learned how hot my work was getting, he tried to hire me. When I refused, he had his own team of scientists work on superconductivity, freely stealing my research. At one point, the spies discovered I thought there might be some value in working in Antarctica, so Pless flew his scientists down to the Voboskov base. He had been using the base for other research, compliments of some greedy Russian bureaucrats."

"And they had good results," Frank guessed.

"Yes, they did," Weinhardt said. "But they didn't understand why exactly."

"So they needed you," Joe said.

"That's right," Weinhardt said. "By this time, I had left Los Alamos. Pless approached me again about working for him, and again I refused. So he called in his precious KGB men. They faked my death, kidnapped me, and brought me to Antarctica. He kicked out the other scientists except for Gregor, who's quite bright but also unscrupulous."

"Were you really working down here?" Frank asked.

"Yes, I was," Weinhardt said. "I knew Pless would kill me eventually, but I was concerned about my wife and Irene. Pless said he would kill them, too, if I didn't come up with results. I tried several times to radio or phone for help, but every time one of Pless's men found me. If you boys had not come for me, I doubt I would have ever left Antarctica."

"You can thank your daughter for that," Frank said as the wind howled even louder.

"I certainly will," Weinhardt said.

Two hours later, the windstorm abated, and an hour after that, three U.S. Navy choppers descended on Voboskov. The choppers evacuated everyone to the U.S. Palmer station on the Antarctic Peninsula. The Voboskov men were held captive there while arrangements were immediately made to send the Hardys and Kenneth Weinhardt back to the States.

Another U.S. Navy chopper had found the lifeless body of Jonathan Pless lying beside a snowmobile about a half mile from Voboskov. Apparently the Swiss executive preferred to take his chances with the elements rather than go to prison for what would surely have been a lengthy stay. His cause of death was hypothermia, otherwise known as freezing to death.

At the Hardys' request, the U.S. Navy contacted Special Agent Martinez in New Mexico. With the assistance of Irene Weinhardt, Martinez and his men were able to collar the two ex-KGB agents with glasses and put them in jail. Then Irene flew back to Bayport so she would be there when her father finally returned home.

Joe glanced out the window of a U.S. Navy LC-130 airplane as it blasted away from the Antarctic Peninsula. He noticed a vast colony of penguins on the white surface and before long was flying over the ice-speckled ocean.

"Something just occurred to me," Frank called to Weinhardt over the plane's roar. "How close were you to making your breakthrough in superconductivity?"

"Rather close," Weinhardt called back. "However, in the world of science, 'rather close' can mean another twenty years before you actually solve the problem. And I'm afraid I would have to return to Antarctica to do it."

"I'm sure the U.S. government would be happy to accommodate you at one of their Antarctic stations," Joe called from across the aisle.

"I'm sure they would," Weinhardt said with a big smile. "And maybe someday I'll come to an agreement with them. But right now all I want is my family around me and perhaps a little pleasant weather. There's always time to change the world."

"Hang in there, Professor," Frank said, shifting in his seat. "Back home it will be spring soon, and you can bask in a temperature way above zero."

"Not to mention absolute zero," Joe added. He turned back to the window and spotted an iceberg rising ominously from the gray water below. Then Joe stretched out in his seat, hoping to catch some sleep and maybe even dream about the upcoming baseball season.

Frank and Joe's next case:

The Hardys have come to Montana to enjoy the challenges of the Big Bison River. Owen Watson runs a river-rafting outfit, and Frank and Joe are eager to test their skills. But their first day out on the fierce white waters turns into a life-and-death struggle when Owen falls victim to a sniper's bullet! Finding out who tried to kill Owen won't be easy. Especially since Joe can't take his eyes off Owen's beautiful daughter. But a wake-up call in the form of a firebomb brings him back to his senses . . . and back into battle. It's a war over the environment, and the Hardys are sitting on a powder keg that's ready to explode at any moment . . . in *River Rats,* Case #122 in The Hardy Boys Casefiles™.